BETRAYAL

KARIN ALVTEGEN is one of Scandinavia's most acclaimed and bestselling crime writers. She was born in Jönköping, Sweden, in 1965 and had a varied career, including work in set design for film and stage, before she started to write. She won Sweden's most prestigious crime novel award, the Glass Key, for *Missing*. Her novel *Shadow* was shortlisted for the CWA International Dagger 2009. She is the great-niece of Astrid Lindgren (author of the *Pippi Longstocking* series), and lives in Stockholm. Her books have been translated into 27 languages.

STEVEN T. MURRAY has been translating from Nordic languages for over thirty years. He is the prize-winning translator of Henning Mankell's *Kurt Wallander* books.

Also by Karin Alvtegen

Missing
Shame
Shadow

KARIN ALVTEGEN

BETRAYAL

CANONGATE

Edinburgh · London · New York · Melbourne

First published in Great Britain in 2005 by
Canongate Books Ltd, 14 High Street,
Edinburgh EH1 1TE
Originally published in Sweden as *Svek* in 2003 by
Natur och Kultur, Stockholm
Published by arrangement with the Salomonssen agency

This paperback edition published in 2011 by Canongate Books

2

British Library Cataloguing-in-Publication Data
A catalogue record for this book is available on
request from the British Library

ISBN 978 0 85786 164 1

Typeset in Sabon by
Palimpsest Book Production Ltd,
Falkirk, Stirlingshire
Printed and bound in Great Britain by
Clays Ltd, St Ives plc

www.canongate.tv

'I don't know.'

Three words.

Each by itself or in some other context completely harmless. Utterly without intrinsic gravity. Merely a statement that he was not sure and therefore chose not to reply.

I don't know.

Three words.

As an answer to the question she had just asked it was a threat to her entire existence. A sudden chasm that opened in the newly polished parquet living-room floor.

She hadn't actually asked the question, she had only spoken the words to make him understand how worried she was. If she asked the question about the unthinkable, then things could only be better afterwards. A shared turning point. The past year had been an eternal struggle, and her question was a way of talking about the fact that she couldn't cope with being strong any longer, couldn't carry the whole burden by herself. She needed his help.

He had given the wrong answer.

Used three words that she had never perceived as an option.

'Do you mean that you're actually questioning our future together?'

I don't know.

There was no follow-up question; his reply eradicated in one single instant all the words she had ever learned. Her brain was forced to do a 180 and re-evaluate everything it had previously known to be beyond all doubt.

The idea that the two of them might not share the future together was not part of her belief system.

Axel, the house, becoming grandma and grandpa together someday.

What words could she possibly find to lead them beyond this moment?

He sat silently on the sofa with his eyes fixed on an American sitcom and his fingers flicking over the remote. Not for an instant had he looked at her since she came into the room, not even when he answered her question. The distance between them was so great that she might not even hear it if he said anything else.

But she did. Clearly and distinctly she heard:

'Did you buy milk on the way home?'

He didn't look at her this time either. Only wondered if she had bought milk on her way home.

A pressure across her chest. And then that prickling down her left arm that she sometimes got when there wasn't enough time.

'Can't you turn off the TV?'

He looked down at the remote and changed the channel. The traffic report.

All of a sudden she realised that a stranger was sitting on her sofa.

He looked familiar, but she didn't know him. He reminded her a great deal of the man who was the father of her son and with whom she had once, more than eleven years earlier, promised God to share both good times and bad until death did them part. The man with whom she had paid off that sofa this past year.

It was the future, theirs and Axel's, that he was calling into question, and he couldn't even show her the respect to turn off the traffic report and look at her.

She was feeling bad now, sick with dread at the question she would have to ask to be able to breathe again.

She swallowed. How would she dare know?

'Have you met someone else?'

Finally he looked at her. His gaze was full of accusation but at least he was looking at her.

'No.'

She closed her eyes. At least there wasn't another woman. She tried desperately to keep herself afloat on his comforting reply. It was all so inconceivable. The room looked just the way it always did, but everything was suddenly different. She looked at the framed photograph she took last Christmas. Henrik in a Santa Claus cap and an excited Axel in the midst of a colourful pile of Christmas presents. The whole family gathered in her childhood home. Three months ago.

'How long have you felt this way?'

He was watching TV again.

'I don't know.'

'Well, approximately? Is it two weeks or two years?'

It seemed an eternity before he answered.

'About a year, I suppose.'

A year. For a year he had gone around questioning their shared future. Without saying a word.

During their vacation last summer when they drove to Italy. During all the dinners with their friends. When he accompanied her on a business trip to London and they made love. The whole time he had been wondering whether he wanted to keep on living with her or not.

She looked at the photograph again. His smiling eyes that met hers through the camera lens. I don't know if I want you any more, if I still want to live with you.

Why hadn't he said anything?

'But why? And how did you think we could work this out?'

He shrugged his shoulders slightly and sighed.

'We don't have fun any more.'

She turned and walked towards the bedroom, couldn't bear to hear any more.

She stood with her back against the closed bedroom door. Axel's calm, secure breathing. Always in the middle, like a link between them, night after night. An assurance and a commitment that they belonged together forever.

Mother, father, child.

There was no alternative.

We don't have fun any more.

He was sitting out there on the sofa with her whole life in his hands. What channel would he choose? He had just taken away control over her life; what she wanted didn't matter, everything was up to him.

Without getting undressed she crawled under the covers, lay down next to the little body and felt the panic grow.

How was she going to resolve this?

And then the numbing weariness. Utterly exhausted from always being the one who took responsibility, who was efficient, who got everything moving and saw to it that what had to be done got done. At the very beginning of their relationship they had assumed their roles. Back then they had laughed at it sometimes, joking about their differences. Over the years the wheel ruts had worn so deep that it was impossible to turn; it was barely possible to get up and look over the edge any longer. She did what had to be done first, and then what she really wanted to do if there was any time left over. He did just the opposite. And by the time he had done what he wanted to do, whatever had to be done was already done. She envied him. She would love to be able to act like that. But then everything would collapse. All she knew was that she felt an indescribable longing for him to take over the helm once in a while. Allow her to sit down for a while so she could rest. Be allowed to lean on *him* for a while.

Instead he sat out there on their recently paid-off sofa and watched the traffic report and put their shared future into question because he wasn't having fun anymore. As if she were going around cheering with joy about their life. But at least she tried, they did have a child together, God damn it!

How had it come to this? When did the moment occur? Why hadn't he told her how he felt? Once they had had a good time together. She had to make him

see that things could be like that again, if only they
didn't give up.

But how was she going to cope?

The sound from the TV was turned off. Expectantly
she listened to his footsteps approaching the
bedroom door. And then the disappointment when
without slowing down they continued on towards his
office.

There was only one thing she wanted.

Only one thing.

That he would come into the room and hold her
and tell her that everything would be back to normal.
That they would get through this together, that everything they had succeeded in building up over all these
years was worth fighting for. That she didn't have to
worry.

He never came.

He knew it the moment she came into the room. She had been following him through the house in recent months, trying to get a conversation started, but somehow he always managed to evade it. It would be so easy just to keep quiet, keep hiding in the everyday atrophy and avoid taking the step into the abyss.

Now it was too late. Now she was standing there blocking the way into his asylum in the office, and this time he didn't stand a chance.

How could he ever tell her the truth? What words would he dare use to speak of it? And then that paralysing fear. Fear of what he knew, fear of what it would mean, and fear of her reaction. He wondered if she could hear his heart pounding, how it was trying to fight its way out and flee to avoid being forced to reveal what was hidden inside.

And then her question that started the ball rolling.

'Do you mean that you're actually questioning our future together?'

Yes! Yes! Yes!

'I don't know.'

He hated the fear, and he hated the fact that she was the one who provoked it. He couldn't even look at her. He was suddenly struck by the realisation that she disgusted him. Disgusted him because she had stood like a rock by his side the past few years as he slowly sank deeper and deeper into despair. She made everything keep on rolling as usual, as if it made no difference that he scarcely participated any more. Yet all she succeeded in doing was to make him feel like a helpless little boy.

Always so fast. Everything finished and ready before he even managed to see that it needed to be done. Always ready to solve every problem, even those that were none of her concern, before he even had a chance to think about it. Like an impatient steam locomotive she charged ahead, trying to make everything right. But it was *not* possible to fix everything. The more he tried to demonstrate how distant he felt, the more zealously she made sure it wouldn't be noticed. And with each day that passed he had grown more conscious that it really didn't matter what he did. She didn't need him any more.

Maybe she never had.

He was merely something that had been hooked onto the locomotive for the journey.

Not for one second had she understood how he really felt. That the boredom and predictability were slowly but surely suffocating him. Half his life was gone, and this was how the rest of it was going to look. There would never be anything more than this. The hour had arrived when it was impossible to postpone any longer everything he wanted to do. Everything he had always planned on doing someday. Well, someday was here now. All the dreams and expectations that he had obediently pushed aside were beginning to cry out, asking him more and more urgently what they should do. Should they leave him or did he want them to stay, and, if so, why? Why should they stick around when he didn't intend to fulfil a single one of them?

He thought about his parents. They sat there in Katrineholm in their house that was all paid off. Everything finished and settled. One evening after another, side by side in their two well-used TV recliners. All conversation had long since stopped. All consideration, all expectation, all respect, everything had slowly but surely died a natural death years ago from lack of nourishment. The only thing remaining was a mutual reproach for all they had missed, all that had been lost to them. The fact that they hadn't been able to give each other more and that many years ago it was already too late. Twenty metres from their easy chairs were the train tracks, and every hour, year after year, the trains had passed that could have taken them away from there. By now they had come to terms with the fact that their own trains had left long ago, although other trains would continue thundering past, rattling the always sparkling glass in their living-room window. They had never purchased a summer cabin, although the income from the sale of Father's car dealership would easily have permitted it. They never took a trip. As if a purely physical displacement might pose some kind of threat to their lives. It was a long time since they had managed to get up and drive the hundred kilometres to Stockholm. They hadn't even come on Axel's sixth birthday; they just sent a belated birthday card with their signatures and a folded hundred-krona bill. Instead of participating in family gatherings they would stay at home and wallow in their feelings of inferiority, prompted by

Eva's well-to-do parents with their academic degrees and intellectual friends. Imprisoned in their own lives they stayed where they were, bitter and careworn.

As if they had each been permanently taken hostage by the other, terrified of being alone.

Out of the corner of his eye he saw her standing motionless in the living room. The sound of the TV came intermittently, like a pulse in synch with his heartbeat.

He felt a desperate need to buy some time, cling to something that was still anchored in his old routines.

'Did you buy milk on the way home?'

She didn't answer. Fear throbbed in his stomach. Why hadn't he just kept his mouth shut?

'Can't you turn off the TV?'

His index finger reacted automatically but pressed the wrong button. A second of hesitation and his reptilian brain decided not to try again. The feeling of suddenly not obeying pushed the fear aside. He was the one holding the control.

'Have you met someone else?'

'No.'

His lips formed his reply by themselves. Like a projecting rock ledge in the plunge towards the abyss. What was he going to do there? On a ledge halfway between being in one place or the other.

'How long have you felt this way?'

'I don't know.'

'Well, approximately? Is it two weeks or two years?'

As long as I can remember, it seems like.

'About a year, I suppose.'

How would he ever dare explain? How would he ever have the courage to take the words in his mouth?

What would happen when he told her that for seven months he was somewhere else every second of the day?

With *her*.

She who had utterly unexpectedly come storming into his heart and given him a reason to want to get up in the morning. Who gave him back his desire and his will. She who opened up all the doors inside him that he had barred shut long ago and who managed to find keys to rooms he didn't even know existed. Who saw him as he really was, made him want to laugh again, want to live. Who made him feel desirable, intelligent, energetic.

Worth loving.

'But why? And how did you think we could work this out?'

He didn't know, didn't even need to lie. In the bedroom lay his six-year-old son. How could he ever do what he really wanted to do and still be able to look him in the eye again?

And how would he ever be able to look himself in the eye again if he stayed and said no to the enormous love he had found?

Hatred passed through him for a moment. If it weren't for her standing there a few metres away from him in the living room, then he could . . .

Full of accusations she would succeed in turning all the joy he felt into shame and guilt. Defile it. Make it seem base and ugly.

All he wanted was to be able to feel what it was like to live again.

'We don't have fun any more.'

He could hear how stupid that sounded. Fucking shit. She always made him feel inferior.

Her gaze felt like a physical accusation. He couldn't move.

An eternity passed before she finally gave up and went towards the bedroom.

He leaned back and closed his eyes.

One single thing he wanted.

Only one.

That *she* would be here with him, hold him tight and say that everything was going to be all right.

For the moment he was saved, but only temporarily.

Starting now, their home was a minefield.

'Is there anything else you need tonight?'

It was the night nurse standing in the doorway. One hand held a tray of pill cups and her other had a firm grip on the door handle. She looked stressed.

'No thanks, we'll be fine now. Isn't that right, Anna?'

The last dregs of gruel ran through the probe into her stomach, and he stroked her brow lightly. The night nurse hesitated for a moment and gave him a quick smile.

'Good night, then. And don't forget that Dr Sahlstedt wants to talk to you before you leave in the morning.'

How could he forget that? It was clear that she didn't know him.

'No, I won't forget.'

She smiled again and closed the door behind her. She was new on the ward and he didn't know her name. There was a lot of turnover of personnel, and he had given up trying to remember their names. Secretly he was grateful that the hospital was chronically short-staffed. At first his constant presence had aroused irritation among the staff, but for the past year they had shown greater appreciation. Sometimes they even took it for granted, and once when he got stuck in traffic and was delayed, they forgot to change the bulging catheter bag. That made him even more aware that without him she would never get the rehabilitation she needed. If they couldn't even remember to change the bag.

He pulled over the bed table on wheels and turned on the radio. The Metropolitan Mix. He was sure that somewhere inside behind her closed eyes she could hear the music he played for her. And he didn't want her to miss out on anything. So that on the day she woke up she would recognise all the new songs that had come out. Since the accident.

He took the skin lotion out of the bedside table, drew a white stripe along her left leg and began to massage it. With even strokes he worked up from the calf, across the knee, and further towards the groin.

'Today it was really fine weather outside. I took a walk down to Årstaviken and sat for a while in the sun by the boat club, there on our wharf.'

He carefully lifted her leg, put one hand behind her knee and bent it cautiously several times.

'Good, Anna . . . Just think, later when you get well we can go down there together again. Take some coffee with us and a blanket and just sit there in the sun.'

He straightened out her leg and placed it on the sheet.

'And all your potted plants are fine; the hibiscus has even started to bloom again.'

He rolled down the bed rails to reach her right hand. The fingers on her left hand had stiffened into a claw, and every day he checked the right one carefully to make sure it hadn't done the same. So that she would be able to continue painting her pictures when she woke up.

He turned off the radio and began to get undressed.

The calm he had longed for began to spread through him. A whole night's sleep.

Nowhere else but here with Anna did the compulsion vanish completely and leave his thoughts in peace. His sanctuary, where he was finally allowed to rest.

Only Anna was strong enough to make him dare resist. With her he felt safe.

Alone he didn't have a chance.

He was only allowed to sleep here once a week, and he had had to nag them about it. Sometimes he was afraid that the privilege would be taken away from him, even though it was no extra trouble for the staff. The new ones especially, like the nurse tonight, seemed to think it was odd. It bothered him a little; was it so strange that they wanted to sleep together? Good Lord, they loved each other, after all.

In any case, he didn't care what they thought.

He thought about the conversation he would have with Dr Sahlstedt in the morning and hoped that it wasn't about the nights he slept with Anna. If they were taken away he would be lost.

He folded his jeans and T-shirt and put them in a neat stack on the visitor's chair. Then he clicked off the bed lamp. The sound of the respirator was more noticeable in the dark. Calm, regular breaths. Like a faithful friend in the dark.

He lay down cautiously beside her, pulled the covers over them, and cupped his hand over one breast.

'Good night, my darling.'

Gently he pressed his crotch against her left thigh and felt the preposterous arousal.

He wanted only one thing.

Only one.

That she would wake up and touch him. Take hold of him. And afterwards she would hold him tight and tell him that he never had to be alone again. That he didn't have to be afraid any more.

He would never leave her.

Never ever.

Axel seemed to know something was wrong. As if the words they had said the night before had polluted the air. They floated like an evil-smelling menace in the house and made her lose her courage as soon as he refused to put on the striped T-shirt.

She had to pull herself together. Not lose control. He hadn't actually said he wanted a divorce, after all, he hadn't done that. Just that he didn't think they had fun any more.

She hadn't been able to sleep. She lay wide awake and listened to his fingers tapping on the keyboard in the office, sometimes hesitant, sometimes determined. How could he just sit down and work? She wondered what kind of article he was writing and realised that she had no idea. It had been a long time since they had talked about his work. As long as he sent out invoices and money came in so she could pay the bills, there hadn't seemed to be any reason.

Always so pressed for time.

For a while she had thought about going in to him and asking, but then she changed her mind. He was the one who should come to her.

Not until around three o'clock did she hear the bedroom door being carefully opened, and he slipped into his side of the double bed.

Axel like a defensive wall between them.

There were only a few minutes left until the meeting as she parked outside the day-care centre. Axel was still in a bad mood, even though she tried to divert his attention as best she could during the drive over. It would be terrible when she left. Axel's sobbing face behind the window-pane.

How could she cope with that today?

She ran into Daniel's father on the way in.

'Hi, Eva, great to see you, I was going to call you two today. We're having that dinner party on the 27th like we said. Can you still come?'

'Yes, I think so.'

He glanced quickly at his watch and kept talking as he backed towards his car.

'We were thinking of inviting the couple that just moved in down the street as well; you know, the house where that old couple used to live. I don't remember their names.'

'I know who you mean. So someone has moved into the place now?'

'Yes, and I think they have kids the same age as ours, so we thought we'd do something neighbourly right away. It's good to have some place within crawling distance when you go out for dinner.'

He laughed at his own joke and took another look at his watch.

'Damn. I've got to be at a meeting on Kungsholmen in fifteen minutes. Why can't they ever start half an hour later?'

He gave a deep sigh.

'Well, then. Say hi to the family.'

He got into his car and she pulled open the door for Axel.

It was always such a rush. Kids who'd just woken up and stressed-out parents who even before they made it to work were worrying about everything they wouldn't have a chance to get done before they had to rush back and pick up their kids on time. Everyone always in a breathless race, with the clock as their worst enemy.

Was it really supposed to be like this?

They walked through the doors and Kerstin came out from the play-room to meet them.

'Hi Axel. Hi Eva.'

'Hi.'

Axel didn't reply but turned his back and stood there with his forehead pressed against the cabinet. She was grateful that it was Kerstin who greeted her today, because she was the one on the staff she knew best. Since Axel's first day five years ago, Kerstin had worked as both day-care teacher and director, with an enthusiasm for her work that never flagged. Driven by devotion, as if she could change the world by constantly reminding the children in her care about the importance of empathy and what was right and wrong. Eva was full of admiration and had often been amazed at Kerstin's energy, especially in view of how exhausted she often felt herself. But on the other hand, Kerstin's own children were in their twenties, so maybe that was the difference.

The clock was her worst enemy.

She remembered her involvement as the head of the student council in high school; Greenpeace, Amnesty, the burning will to change things. And she remembered how it felt when she still had the conviction that what was wrong could be fixed, injustices could cease, and if she only put in enough time and energy then the world could be changed. Back then her outrage over the unjust imprisonment of a person on the other side of the globe would make her start petition drives and organise demonstrations. Now that she was grown up and really could do something, she was grateful if she managed to get to a day-care parents' meeting that affected her own son. The desire to change the world had been precipitately transformed into a hope that there would be enough hours in the day – her outrage into a deep sigh and some guilty spare change in the Red Cross collection box at the grocery store. All to silence her guilty conscience. Always new decisions to make. What telephone plan to sign up with, which electrical company would be most advantageous, where to invest the pension money, which school was the best, which family doctor, the lowest interest on the mortgage. And they all affected her little world: what was best and most beneficial for her and her family. Endless decisions to make, and you still never knew if you had made the right ones. Everyone thinking of themselves first. When all mandatory decisions had been made, there was no energy left to make a stand on the issues that really should matter. The ones that could change what really should be changed. She remembered the ironic sticker she had had on her notice-board in her bedroom when she was a girl: 'Of course I take a stand on all the injustices in the world. I've said 'bloody hell' many times!' She would never be like that. Or so she had thought back then.

'Are you angry today?'

Axel didn't answer Kerstin's question, and Eva went over and squatted down by his side.

'It wasn't a good morning. Isn't that right, Axel?'

Filippa and her mother came in the door and Kerstin's attention was diverted to them instead.

Eva pulled Axel close and held him tight.

Everything's going to be all right. You don't have to be afraid. I promise I'll work this out.

'Hey Axel, the meeting's starting now, everyone else is already inside. Come on, let's go in. Today it's your turn to get the fruit from the kitchen.'

Kerstin reached out her hand to him, and he finally gave in, went over to his corner and hung up his jacket. Eva stood up.

'Henrik will pick him up at four.'

Kerstin smiled and nodded, took Axel by the hand, and went into the play-room. Eva followed along behind. Actually she might be the one who was having the hardest time saying goodbye today. Axel let go of Kerstin's hand and ran over to Linda, one of the other day-care teachers, and climbed up on her knee.

Gratefully she felt the worst of her worries recede. It was Axel's everyday world she saw before her, and until she fixed all the problems at least he was having a good time here. Linda stroked Axel's hair and gave her a quick smile.

Eva smiled back.

Here he was safe.

Jonas got to his appointment with Dr Sahlstedt early. He had been waiting for more than fifteen minutes when the doctor came hurrying down the corridor and opened the door to his office.

'Sorry you had to wait, I had to look at a patient down in intensive care. Come in.'

He closed the door behind them and went over to sit down at his desk.

Jonas just stood there. Anna's calm seemed to be blown away, the compulsion was well aware that he was defenceless now, and soon it would grow strong enough. Now he would have to pay for last night's peace and quiet. He had felt the signals even when he was waiting in the corridor. A creeping unrest that had begun during the morning rounds. The looks from the staff over Anna's sleeping body. No specific word, but rather a new tone of voice, a vague insinuation.

'Please have a seat.'

He felt the pressure growing, taking over bit by bit.

Four steps forward to the visitor's chair. Not three or five. Or else he would have to go back to the door and start over. Three and five had to be avoided at all costs.

Without touching the chair's armrest he sat down and followed Sahlstedt's hand with his gaze, the way it pulled over a brown folder but then rested on the closed casebook.

Dr Sahlstedt looked at him in silence.

Was it really four steps he had taken? He was no longer sure. Good Lord. Alingsås to Arjeplog 1179 kilometres, Arboga to Arlanda 144, Arvidsjaur to Borlänge 787.

'How are you doing?'

The unexpected question took him by surprise. He knew that the compulsion couldn't be seen on the surface. After all these years he had developed an exceptional ability to conceal his inner inferno.

As well as the shame over his weakness at not being able to control it.

'Fine, thank you.'

Silence. If it was true that the doctor facing him actually was interested in the state of his health, then it was obvious that the reply had not satisfied him. There was a grave look in his eyes. An ominous gravity that made it clear that the conversation they were going to have was something more than just a normal report.

Jonas shifted his position in the chair. Don't touch the armrests.

'How old are you, Jonas?'

He swallowed. Not five. Not even with a two in front of it.

'I'll be twenty-six next year. Why do you ask? I thought we were going to talk about Anna.'

Dr Sahlstedt regarded him and then looked down at the table.

'It's not about Anna any longer. It's about you.'

Borlänge to Boden 848, Borås to Båstad 177.

'What . . . I don't know what you mean.'

Sahlstedt raised his eyes again.

'What kind of job did you have? Before all this happened, I mean.'

'I was a postman.'

He nodded with interest.

'I see. Do you ever miss your colleagues from work?'

Was he toying with him? Or maybe postmen worked in flocks in the high-class neighbourhood where he imagined Dr Sahlstedt lived.

The doctor in front of him gave a little sigh when he got no answer and opened the brown casebook.

Had he really not brushed against the armrest when he sat down? He was no longer certain. If he had, he would have to touch it again to neutralise the first time he touched it. But what if he hadn't touched it? Good Lord, he had to neutralise it somehow.

'You've been on sick leave for almost two and a half years now. As long as Anna has been here.'

'Yes.'

'Why is that, actually?'

'What do you think? So I can be here with Anna, of course.'

'Anna can get along here without you. The staff will take care of her.'

'You know as well as I do that they don't have time to work with her as much as necessary.'

Dr Sahlstedt suddenly looked sad; he sat quietly and looked down at his hands. The silence was about to drive Jonas crazy. With all his might he tried to resist the compulsion's rage which was going berserk inside his body.

The doctor looked up at him again.

'Necessary for what, Jonas?'

He couldn't answer. The wash basin was on the wall to his left. He had to go and wash his hands. Had to wash away the touch if he had indeed happened to touch the armrest.

'As you know, the fever is not going down, and we did a new EKG yesterday. The infection in the aortic valve is not subsiding. At regular intervals it's releasing small septic embolisms, small particles, one might say, filled with bacteria. These bacteria go straight up to her brain stem, and that's why she continues to be struck by new blood clots in the brain.'

'I see.'

'This is the third clot she has had in two months. And with each new one her level of consciousness drops.'

He had heard things like this before. The doctors always told him the worst so as not to give him false hopes.

'You have to try and accept that she will never wake up from her coma.'

He could no longer fight it, and he stood up and went over to the wash basin.

Four steps. Not three.

He had to wash his hands.

'There is nothing more we can do to help her. Deep inside you know that too, don't you?'

He let the water run over his hands. Closed his eyes and felt the relief when the pressure eased.

'You have to start to let go now. Try to move on.'

'She reacted when I massaged her this morning.'

Dr Sahlstedt sighed behind his back.

'I'm sorry, Jonas. I know how hard you've struggled to help her, and we all have. But it could be a matter of weeks or months now, we don't know. In the worst case she could remain like this for another year.'

In the worst case.

He let the water run. Stood with his back to the man who claimed to be Anna's doctor. Ignorant idiot. How could he claim to know what was moving inside her? How many times had *he* massaged her legs? Sat next to her and tried to straighten out her crooked fingers? Brought her perfume and fruit to keep her sense of smell alive? Never. The only thing he had done was to hook up some wires to her skull, press a button, and then draw the conclusion that she was incapable of feeling anything.

'Why does she react then?'

Dr Sahlstedt sat in silence for a moment.

'I've been trying for a long time to get you to talk with some of our . . . some of my colleagues here at the Karolinska Institute, but . . . now I've actually taken the liberty of making an appointment for you. I'm convinced that it could help you get through this. You have your whole life ahead of you, Jonas. I don't think that Anna would want you to spend it here at the hospital.'

The sudden fury came like a liberator. The compulsion died down and retreated to the side.

He shut off the tap, took two paper towels, and turned around.

'You just said that she couldn't feel anything. Then why would she care about that?'

Dr Sahlstedt sat utterly still. A sudden beep from his breast pocket broke the silence.

'I have to go. We'll talk more another day. You have an appointment with Yvonne Palmgren tomorrow morning at 8.15.'

He tore off a yellow Post-It note from the pad and held it out to him. Jonas stood motionless.

'Jonas, it's for your own good. Maybe it's time you started thinking a little about yourself.'

Dr Sahlstedt gave up and stuck the note on the desk top before he went out the door. Jonas just stood there. Talk to a psychiatrist! What about? She would try to get into his thoughts, and why should he permit that? He'd been so successful at keeping everyone away from them up till now.

Anna was the only one he had let in.

She was his and he was hers. That's how it would always be. For two years and five months he had devoted all his time to making her well again. Trying to make everything all right. And now they wanted to get him to accept the fact that it had all been in vain.

Nobody was going to take her away from him.

Nobody.

When he came outside it had started to rain. On the nights he spent at the hospital he always took public transport because the parking fees were so high. They charged round the clock, and he couldn't afford it any more. He buttoned up his jacket and walked towards the subway.

He was terrified of the night, well aware of what was waiting. It was in the loneliness of his apartment that the control took over. The constantly nagging feeling that there was something important he had forgotten. The tap in the bathroom, had he turned it off properly? And the gas rings on the cooker? And what about the door, did he really lock it? Then the temporary calm when he had checked that everything was as it should be. But what if he had bumped into the light switch in the bathroom when he walked past without noticing it? Maybe he had managed to turn on the cooker just as he was checking that it was off. And he was no longer sure that he had locked the door. Had to check again.

The simplest thing was to stay away. Then he knew that everything was under control. Before he left the apartment he always turned off all the gas rings, unplugged the cords of all the electrical appliances and devices, and wiped the dust off the plugs. One never knew if a spark might start a fire. He stored the remote control for the TV in a drawer; it absolutely mustn't be left out on the table so that a ray of sunlight through the window might strike the sensor and make it catch fire.

And then going out the door. For the past six months the locking ritual had become so complicated that he had to write it down on a piece of paper he kept in his wallet to make sure he didn't miss something.

He stood down on the street looking up at the black windows of the flat. A man in his fifties he had never seen before came out the front door and gave him a suspicious look. He couldn't bring himself to go up to the flat. Instead he took his keyring from his pocket and got into his car, turned the ignition and let the engine idle.

Only with Anna was he left in peace. Only she was strong enough to vanquish the annihilating fear.

And now they thought he would just let go and move on.

Where to?

Where was it they wanted him to go?

She was all he had.

It was after the accident that it started again. It came sneaking up, lying in wait for him, at first only as a diffuse need to create symmetry and restore balance. And later, when the gravity of her injuries had become more and more obvious, the pressure to perform the complicated rituals had intensified to an inescapable compulsion. The only way to neutralise the threat was to give in. If he didn't obey the impulses properly, something horrible would happen. What, he didn't know, only that the fear and pain grew intolerable if he tried to fight back.

When he was a teenager it had been different. Then the pressure eased if he just avoided touching door handles with his hands or walked backwards down the stairs or touched all the lampposts he passed. Back then it had been easier to handle, when it was possible to hide behind the self-centredness of a teenager.

No one knew, either now or then, and well aware of the insanity of what he was doing he had invented tricks and gestures to make the compulsory rituals look like a natural part of his behaviour.

Every day a secret war.

Only during the year with Anna had he been free.

He loved Anna. He would never leave her.

His mobile rang in his jacket pocket. He took it

out and looked at the display. No number. Two rings.
He had to answer after the fourth or forget it.

It might be Karolinska Hospital.

'Jonas.'

'It's Pappa.'

Not now. Damn.

'You've got to help me, Jonas.'

He was drunk. Drunk and sad. And Jonas knew
why he was calling. It had been eight months since
the last time he called, and it had been the same story
then. It always was. He probably didn't call more
often to plead with his son because he was seldom
sober enough to remember the number.

Jonas could hear the sound of people in the background. His father was drinking in some bar somewhere.

'I don't have time to talk right now.'

'Damn it, Jonas, you've got to help me. I can't go
on living like this, I can't stand it any more . . .'

His voice broke and there was silence on the line.
Only the murmur of voices.

Jonas leaned back against the headrest and closed
his eyes. His father had begun to use his tears as a
last resort early on. And frightened by his father's vulnerability, Jonas had tried to be loyal and thus was
forced into betrayal.

He was thirteen years old when it started.

*Just tell her I have to work late tonight. Damn it,
Jonas, you know that this woman . . . well, shit, she
gives a hell of a good ride.*

Thirteen years old and his father's loyal co-
conspirator. The truth, whatever and wherever it was,
had to be kept secret from his mother at all costs.

To protect her.

Year in and year out.

And then the constant question inside him of why his pappa did what he did.

There were plenty of people in town who knew. He remembered all the conversations that would suddenly stop when he and his mamma entered the grocer's and that resumed again as soon as she turned her back. All the sympathetic smiles that were directed at her from neighbours and girlfriends, people she thought were her friends, but who year after year out of sheer cowardice held their tongues about the truth. And he, too, walking beside her and holding his tongue as well, he was the worst traitor of them all. He recalled a conversation he had heard once when she was sitting with a neighbour in the kitchen. His mother thought that he had gone out and didn't hear, but he was lying in bed reading a comic book. He heard her in tears, talking about her suspicions that her husband had met someone else. Heard how she sat there at the kitchen table and overcame her own reservations enough to dare express her shameful misgivings. And the woman lied. Straight into his mamma's face she lied as she accepted coffee and home-baked buns. Lied and said that his mamma was surely just imagining things and that every marriage had its ups and downs and that there was certainly nothing to worry about.

And then the slaps on the back from the men urging his father on to new conquests, and more overtime to keep alive his reputation as an irresistible ladykiller, while Jonas stayed at home covering for him. Constant lies that were compensated for by the growing pressure to perform his rituals to dull the sense of dread.

And then new lies, to hide the compulsion.

How he had wondered about all those women. Who were they, what were they thinking? Did they know that his father had a wife and a son somewhere, waiting for the man they were seducing? Did it mean anything to them? Did they care? What made them give their bodies to a man who only wanted to fuck them and then go home and deny them to his wife?

He never could understand it.

The only thing he knew was that he hated each and every one of them.

Hated them all.

The bubble burst a few months before his eighteenth birthday. Something as trivial as a little lipstick on a shirt collar. After five years of lies the constant betrayal was revealed, and his father had used Jonas's knowledge like a scared rabbit to protect himself from her pain. To avoid bearing all the guilt himself.

She had never been able to forgive either of them.

She was doubly betrayed.

The wound they gave her was so deep that it could never heal.

He had remained in the house in silence after his father moved out, watched her from a distance in the destroyed home. It reeked of shame and hatred. She refused to talk to anyone. In the daytime she seldom left her bedroom, and if she did it was only to go to the toilet. Jonas tried to make up for his betrayal by taking care of shopping for food and other errands, but she never came out to the table when he fixed their meals. Every night at two-thirty he set off on his moped to his job delivering newspapers, and when he came home at six he could see that she had taken something to eat from the refrigerator. The dishes she used stood carefully washed in the dish rack.

But she never spoke a word to him.

'I don't have time to talk now.'

He cut off the connection and leaned over the steering wheel.

This is the third embolism she has had in two months. And each time her level of consciousness drops.

How could she do this to him? What more did she want from him to convince her to stay?

He wouldn't be able to stand the loneliness in the flat. Not tonight.

He looked over his shoulder and backed up. He didn't know where he was going.

Only one thing.

If she didn't touch him soon, he would go crazy.

Eva had a hard time remembering the last time she had left work early, if ever. The biggest advantage of the fact that Henrik worked at home was that he could collect Axel from day-care or dash over there on short notice if the boy was sick. This went without saying ever since she became a partner and also contributed the major part of their common income. But she tried never to get home later than six.

Today she was going to surprise him and come home earlier than usual.

No one could claim that she got very much done that day. With her eyes on structural efficiencies and profitability calculations, the grinding anxiety had constantly intruded on her thoughts. She had a feeling of unreality. He had suddenly put in question the only thing she had never questioned.

The family.

Everything else was replaceable.

She raised her eyes from the computer screen and looked out the window. The only thing she saw was the façade on the other side of Birger Jarlsgatan. Another office full of other people; she had no idea what they were working on, she didn't know a single one of them. Most of the daylight hours, day after day, year after year, they spent thirty metres from each other and saw one another more than they saw their own families.

A nine-hour workday, if she didn't work through lunch, and half an hour's travel time in rush-hour traffic. It gave her scarcely an hour and a half each day with Axel, an hour and a half when he was tired and cranky after eight hours with twenty other children at the day-care centre, and she was tired and cranky after nine hours of demands and stress at her job. And then at eight o'clock, after he went to bed, she and Henrik would have their time together. The grown-up hour. That was when they were supposed to sit in peace and quiet and see to it that their relationship was fantastic, talk about their day, take an interest in each other's work, what had happened, share their thoughts. And then somehow manage to make heartfelt love with each other when they finally tumbled into bed. According to the Sunday supplements, that was how they should ensure their marriage would last. And then, of course, plan short romantic trips and get a babysitter so they could have their own gilt-edged time together. If there had been a slave available who could go grocery shopping, drive Axel to swimming lessons, get involved in the parents' group at the day-care centre, prepare dinner, wash clothes, call the plumber and ask him to fix the leak underneath the kitchen counter, do the ironing, make sure all the bills got paid on time, clean the house, open all the window envelopes and take care of all the family's social contacts, then it might have been possible. What she wanted most of all was to be able to sleep an entire weekend. Undisturbed. To see whether there was any possibility of getting rid of the exhaustion she felt, the weariness that permeated marrow and bone and longed only for things to get done without her participation.

She thought about the seminar the company held last autumn. 'Taking responsibility for your life.' She had felt energised afterwards; many truths had been uttered that sounded so simple though she had never thought of them herself.

Every moment I choose whether I want to be a victim or the creator of my own destiny.

Full of inspiration she had hurried home to tell Henrik about her experience. He had sat silently and listened, but when she offered to get tickets for the next lecture the man would be giving, he wasn't interested.

What would you do if you were told you had six months left to live?

That was the question he opened the seminar with.

When it was over it hung in the air unanswered.

She still had done nothing about finding an answer.

On the way home she took a detour past Östermalms Market Hall, bought two lobsters at Elmqvist's Fish Shop and then continued on to the wine shop on Birger Jarlsgatan.

She had booked the trip during lunch and had the tickets sent by courier to the office.

Everything was going to be fine again.

It was only four thirty when she got home. Axel's

jacket lay flung on the floor inside the front door, and she hung it up on the elephant-shaped hook that she had put up for him at the proper height.

She heard Henrik's voice from the kitchen.

'I have to go now. I'll try to ring you a bit later.'

She took off her coat, hiding the bags with the lobsters and champagne inside the closet, and went up the stairs.

He was sitting at the kitchen table reading *Dagens Nyheter*. Next to him lay the cordless phone.

'Hi.'

'Hi.'

He kept looking at the newspaper. She closed her eyes. Why couldn't he even make an effort? Why did he always leave the responsibility to her?

She tried to push aside her annoyance.

'I came home a little earlier today.'

He raised his head and glanced at the digital clock on the microwave oven.

'I can see that.'

'I thought I'd drive Axel over to Mamma and Pappa's and let him sleep there tonight.'

This time he looked up at her. A quick, embarrassed look.

'Oh? Why?'

She tried to smile.

'I'm not telling. You'll see.'

For an instant she thought he looked almost scared.

'Axel!'

'I have to work tonight.'

'Axel! Do you want to stay at Grandma and Grandpa's tonight?'

Quick steps came running from the living room.

'Yes!'

'Come on then, let's get you packed.'

The familiar drive out to Saltsjöbaden took only fifteen minutes. Axel sat quietly and expectantly in the back seat, and the temporary calm was enough for her to realise that she was nervous. She and Henrik hadn't slept together since they were in London, and that was almost ten months ago. She actually hadn't thought about it before now. Neither of them had taken the initiative and so neither of them had been rejected. They probably just hadn't felt like it, it was no worse than that. And of course Axel always slept between them.

She drove up and parked on the paved driveway. Axel jumped out of the car and ran the short distance up to the porch.

She looked at her childhood home through the windscreen. Large and secure, the yellow turn-of-the-century house with its white gingerbread trim stood where it had always stood, surrounded by gnarled, well-pruned apple trees. In a couple of months they would be covered with white blossoms.

In a couple of months.

By then everything would be back to normal.

All she had to do was muster enough energy to fight a little harder.

Suddenly it occurred to her that she had to ring up the garage and make an appointment to have the winter tyres removed.

The front door opened and Axel disappeared inside. Eva climbed out of the car, took Axel's bag from the back seat and went towards the house.

Her mother came out on the porch.

'Hi, have you got time for a cup of coffee?'

'No, I have to get back right away. Thanks for being able to take him on such short notice.'

She set the bag on the floor of the entryway and gave her mother a quick hug.

'His toothbrush is in the outside pocket.'

'Did something come up?'

'Yes. Henrik got a new client, so we thought we should celebrate a little.'

'Oh, how nice. Who's the client?'

'It's some kind of series of articles for a big magazine, I don't know exactly. Axel! I'm leaving now.'

'I'll pick him up in the morning. We have to leave by seven thirty if we're going to make it.'

Axel popped up in the doorway, followed by her father.

'Hi, sweetheart. You're not leaving already, are you?'

'Yes, otherwise I won't make it.'

Her mother filled in the lie for her this time.

'Henrik apparently got a great new job that they're going to celebrate.'

'There, you see. You'll have to tell him congratulations from me. And what about you? How did it go with that merger you were having such problems with?'

'Oh, that worked out fine. We managed to push it through at last.'

He stood in silence, smiling. Then he reached out his hand and put it on Axel's head.

'You know, Axel, you have a very talented mamma. When you grow up she'll probably be just as proud of you as we've been of her.'

She suddenly felt like crying. Crawling into his lap and being little again. Not thirty-five and a management consultant and a mother responsible for saving her family. She had always been able to rely on them. A solid foundation. They had always believed in her, supported her, made her believe in her own abilities and that nothing was impossible.

This time there was nothing they could do.

This time she stood utterly alone.

How could she ever admit to them that Henrik might not want to live with their daughter any more. The one they were so proud of, the one who was so talented and strong and successful.

She squatted down in front of Axel and pulled him close to hide her uncertainty.

'I'll pick him up in the morning. Have a great time tonight.'

She forced a smile and went down the steps and over to her car. Through the windscreen she could see them standing on the porch and waving.

Together.

Pappa's arm around Mamma's shoulders. Forty years and they still stood there, side by side, content with their life and so proud of and grateful for their only daughter.

She would like to stand like that someday herself.

It was this childhood home that she wanted to recreate for Axel. The security. A total faith that no matter what happened it would be there.

The family.

Unwavering.

It was what you could always fall back on if everything else went to hell. She had been privileged to grow up that way. With Mamma and Pappa always there if she needed them. Always ready to help out. And the older she got, the less she needed them, as long as she knew they would always be there.

As long as she knew that.

Their boundless faith in her, that she would make it, that she was capable. No matter what she chose to do.

What was wrong with her own generation? Why were they never satisfied? Why did everything and everyone always have to be measured, compared, evaluated? What was this unresolved restlessness that kept driving them onward, forward, to the next goal? A total inability to stop and be happy about the goals they had already reached, a constant fear that someone might pass them by, that they had missed something that might have been slightly better, made them slightly happier. So many choices, but how could they manage all of them?

The older generation had fought to realise their dreams: education, a home, children, and then the goal was attained. None of them had ever suspected that they might need so much more. No one accused them of lacking ambition if they stayed at a job more than a couple of years; on the contrary, loyalty was honourable. They had had the ability to sit down and feel content with their lives. They fought hard and then enjoyed their successes.

She opened the front door as quietly as possible and sneaked into the kitchen, putting the champagne in the freezer. She didn't see Henrik around; the door to his office was closed. A quick shower and then take out the new lacy lingerie she had bought at lunchtime. The nervousness came over her again when she looked at her face in the bathroom mirror. Maybe she ought to make an effort more often. But how would she manage? She took off the silver clasp at the nape of her neck and let her hair fall over her shoulders. He had always liked it best when her hair was down.

For a moment she considered putting on only her robe over the black lingerie, but she didn't dare. Good Lord. Here she was standing in her bathroom where she had stood naked with her family every morning and evening for almost eight years, and she was nervous about asking her husband to come to dinner.

How had it come to this?

She put on black jeans and a jumper.

The door to the office was still closed when she came out. She listened but couldn't hear his fingers on the keyboard. There was utter silence inside. But then suddenly the beep of an email being sent. Maybe he had finished working.

She quickly set the table with the good dishes and was just about to light the candles when he was suddenly standing in the kitchen doorway. He glanced at the festive table setting, but there was no hint of joy in his face.

She smiled at him.

'Would you switch off the big light?'

He hesitated an instant before he turned and did as she asked. She picked up the bottle of champagne, unscrewed the wire, and twisted out the cork. The champagne glasses they had received as a wedding present were already on the table. He was still standing in the doorway, didn't make a move to approach her.

She walked over and handed him a glass.

'Here you are.'

She had heart palpitations now. Why couldn't he help her out? Did he have to make her look ridiculous because she was trying?

She went back and sat down at the table. For a moment she thought he would go back into his office. But then he finally came and sat down.

The silence was like an extra wall in the room. It cut right across the table, with each of them on one side of it.

She looked down at her plate but couldn't eat a bite. On the chair next to her lay the blue plastic folder with the tickets. She wondered if he saw her hand shaking when she handed it to him through the silence.

'This is for you.'

He regarded her outstretched hand suspiciously.

'What is it?'

'Could be something nice. You'll have to look and see.'

He opened the folder as she watched. She knew that he had always wanted to go to Iceland. An adventure holiday. It had never happened. She had preferred holidays in the sun where she could rest, and she was always the one who planned and arranged their holiday trips.

'I thought that Axel could stay with Mamma and Pappa, and we could go alone, just the two of us, for a change.'

He raised his eyes and looked at her, and his eyes

frightened her. Never before had anyone looked at her with such an annihilating coldness. Then he put down the plastic folder on the table and stood up, looked her straight in the eye as if to ensure that each and every word would hit its mark.

'There is nothing, absolutely nothing, that I want to do together with you.'

Every syllable felt like a slap in the face.

'If it weren't for Axel and the house, I would have left long ago.'

Psychotherapist Yvonne Palmgren had insisted that they have what she called 'the first conversation' in Anna's room. Jonas had no objections; in there, at least, the compulsion would leave him in peace. Though he had a hard time understanding what good the conversation would do. But fearing that they might take away the nights he slept over if he didn't co-operate, he had finally agreed to meet with her.

She was sitting in a chair by one of the windows – maybe fifty or fifty-five. Her white smock unbuttoned over a pair of grey trousers and a red jumper. A childish necklace made of big, colourful plastic beads rested on her full bosom, and four felt-tip pens in garish neon colours stuck up from her breast pocket. Maybe all those cheerful colours were intended to outweigh all the blackness she confronted daily in her patients' tormented souls.

He sat down on the edge of Anna's bed and held her right hand that was still normal. He could feel the woman in the chair looking at him. He knew full well what she was thinking.

'Where do you think we should start?'

He turned his head and looked at her.

'No idea.'

He had shown up as agreed; the rest wasn't his

problem, she would have to take care of that. He wasn't the one who needed this conversation, it was the County Council, so that they could terminate Anna's rehabilitation in good conscience and slowly but surely allow her brain to atrophy so that they were spared any more trouble. But they could forget about winning him over to their side.

'Do you think it's annoying to have this conversation?'

He sighed.

'No, not particularly. I just don't understand what the point is.'

'You don't think it's because you're afraid that you might have negative feelings about it?'

He couldn't even manage to answer that. What the hell did she know about fear? Just asking the question meant that she had never even been close to it. Never felt that wild terror of losing everything. To have no power over one's own thoughts, no control of one's own life.

Or Anna's.

'How long had you been together? I mean before the accident.'

'A year.'

'But you weren't actually living together?'

'No. We were just about to get married when . . . when . . .'

He broke off and looked at Anna's closed eyelids.

The woman in the chair shifted position. Braced herself on the armrests and then folded her hands over the open plastic folder on her lap.

'Anna is a bit older than you.'

'Yes.'

Yvonne Palmgren glanced down at her papers.

'Almost twelve years older.'

He sat in silence. Why should he say anything when she could satisfy her sick curiosity by reading it all from the file?

'Can you tell me a little about your relationship? What your life was like before all this happened? You can describe a normal day if you like.'

He stood up and walked over to the window. He hated this. Why should he have to divulge his and Anna's life to a stranger? What right did she have to come trampling into their memories?

'Did you talk about moving in together?'

'We live in the same building. Anna has a studio at the top of the stairs. She's an artist.'

'I see.'

He remembered their first meeting so well. He had distributed the day's mail, gone home and slept for a few hours, and was on his way to Konsum to buy groceries. She was standing in the stairwell on the ground floor, busy loading cartons into the lift. They said hello to each other and he held the door when she went out to the car to fetch the last box. The similarity was striking. How was it possible for anyone to be so similar? He stood there, not wanting to leave before he had a chance to talk with her. Afterwards it was so natural that he had stayed. That he overcame his hesitation and asked whether he could help her. He didn't recall what she replied. He only remembered her smile. A candid, warm smile that made her eyes narrow to slits and made him feel chosen, unique, handsome in someone else's eyes.

He had helped her with the boxes and then she

asked him in to her new studio, and she had shown him round, happy and proud. He had mostly looked at her. There was a kind of radiance about her. A genuine naturalness so attractive that he became quite bewildered. After only five minutes he had known that she was the one he had always been waiting for. That his whole life had been merely leading up to their meeting.

'What did you use to do together?'

The psychotherapist's question dragged him back to the present. He turned towards her.

'Everything.'

'Can you give me an example?'

They started eating their meals together. He would come home from work just in time for lunch, and she worked at home, so after a while it became a habit. One day at her place, the next at his. She was the first person he had allowed in his flat in several years. He had never been able to overcome the distaste he felt at how messy things were after someone visited. She had laughed at his systematic order and claimed that all the right angles made her nervous, finally convincing him to redecorate. She had even run up to her studio and fetched a big oil painting that they hung up in the room. It was after she left that night that he fully realised how much he loved her. He had wandered about in confusion, and yet the compulsion could not reach him. Completely unaware of her improbable feat, she had used her mere presence to neutralise the danger that threatened him.

That night he stood naked in front of the painting and traced her brush-strokes with his finger. The grooved canvas aroused a desire so strong in him that it was painful, but he would not let it go. He would save it and give it to her when she was ready.

'Did you have a lot of friends?'

He turned back to the window and stuffed one hand in his pocket. His memory had revived the wild longing. The hunger of his skin that would drive him crazy if she didn't touch him soon.

'Not particularly.'

'Relatives, then?'

'Her parents died in a car crash when she was fourteen. She was one of those children who's like a dandelion and succeeds in life in spite of everything. Strong and stubborn.'

'Does she have any siblings?'

'A brother, but he lives in Australia.'

'And you?'

He turned his head and looked at her.

'What do you mean?'

'Your parents?'

'What about them?'

'I don't know. Tell me.'

'We have no contact. I moved down to Stockholm when I was eighteen, thought it was good to get away from there.'

'Get away from what?'

'I lived up north of Gävle.'

'Yes, but most people stay in contact with their family even if they move away.'

'I see.'

Nine words his mother had said to him after the betrayal was revealed. Nine words. It was on his eighteenth birthday. He was sitting in the kitchen eating breakfast, had just come home from his paper round. For three months he had done what he could to win her forgiveness, but she had not been receptive. And his father had holed up in a one-room apartment in Gävle to get away from the shame that her boundless sorrow and disappointment had created. He took his clothes and one of the twin beds from the bedroom and disappeared.

Suddenly she was standing there in the kitchen doorway. She was wearing the flowered robe that he knew smelled so good, smelled of Mamma. And he had been filled with joy and thought that maybe, maybe she was ready to forgive him now. Now that it was his birthday and she was standing there in the kitchen doorway.

Nine words she had said.

I don't want you to live here any more.

Yvonne Palmgren shifted position in her chair once again. A couple of papers from her folder started to slip, and she caught them just as they were about to fall to the floor.

He lowered his gaze and went to sit with Anna again.

'Why don't you have any contact with your parents?'

'Because I don't feel like it.'

'Doesn't that ever make you feel empty?'

'No.'

She cleared her throat and closed the folder in her lap.

'I think that will be enough for now, but I would like to continue our conversation this afternoon.'

He shrugged his shoulders. It annoyed him that he was forced to do as they said. That he couldn't just tell them all to go to hell.

'Shall we say two o'clock?'

She got up and went over to the bed, looked at Anna and then at him, and moved towards the door.

'I'll see you then. Goodbye for now.'

He didn't reply.

He saw the door close behind her and took Anna's hand, placed it on his crotch, and closed his eyes.

Never in her life had she felt so alone.

He had slept on the sofa. Took his pillow and quilt and without saying a word he had left her with all the unanswered questions that she couldn't bring herself to ask. His last words at the kitchen table had struck her dumb.

Anxiety like a cramp in her guts.

Why was he so angry? Where did his rage come from? What could she possibly have done to deserve being treated like this?

Alone in the double bed she was sorry that she had let Axel sleep over at her parents' house. She would have given anything to have him here now, hear his breathing, reach out her hand and feel the warm back of his pyjamas.

At four o'clock she couldn't stand it any more. With her face red and swollen and her eyes watering, she pulled on her robe and went out to the living room. It was still dark outside, but in the pale moonlight she could see that he was lying on his back with his arms behind his head. His knees a bit bent, the sofa too short to permit him to stretch out his legs. She wondered briefly why he didn't go and sleep in Axel's bed. A kid's bed, of course, but surely better than the sofa.

She sat down in the armchair, at the very edge.

'Are you asleep?'

He didn't answer.

She pulled her robe tighter around her and shivered. The mullioned windows in the room needed to be puttied again. The electric heater couldn't keep the room warm when most of the heat went straight out through the draughty cracks. It would be a time-consuming job, eight small panes in each window. Maybe they could hire someone and avoid wasting their time during their badly needed holiday. But maybe that was no longer so important.

She swallowed.

'Henrik?'

Not a sound.

'Henrik, dear, can't we just talk a little? Can't you explain to me what's happening?'

He didn't stir.

'Can't you at least explain why you're so angry? What is it I've done?'

He turned over on his side and pulled up the covers. He must have heard from her voice that she had been sad, that she was still sad, but she realised that he was not going to answer even if he did hear her. He intended to shut her out and her questions as if she had never uttered them. She leaned her head back and closed her eyes, trying to stifle the sound of desperation that was lodged like a scream in her throat, demanding to be released. A cornered animal whose every instinct was signalling her to fight, but she didn't know what to defend herself against. For a good while she sat there, unable to get up, but finally she managed to persuade her legs to take her back to the empty double bed.

She had just lain down when she heard him go into the bathroom.

He left her alone.

She didn't fall asleep until after five o'clock. At seven she woke up when the front door closed. She presumed he was going to collect Axel and take him to the day-care centre.

She lay there staring at the second-hand on her wristwatch, unable to move. Step by step it was leading her farther away from reason. How was she going to resolve this?

The sudden ring of the telephone made her gasp. The only reason she decided to pick it up was that it might be him.

'Eva speaking.'

'Hi, it's me.'

'Oh, hi Mamma.'

She lay back down.

'How did it go yesterday?'

'Oh, fine, thanks. Was it all right with Axel?'

'Yes, but he woke up at half past one and was sad and absolutely wanted to ring you even though we told him it was much too late. We tried your mobiles but they were turned off, and your home phone kept giving a busy signal. Were you having a good time?'

Kept giving a busy signal?

'Yes, it was very nice.'

Who had he called so late? Because she hadn't heard the phone ring. And if he was on the line, the call waiting signals should still have gone through.

'Pappa and I thought we'd ask if you two would like to come over for dinner on Sunday. I've got a moose steak left over from this autumn that I thought I'd do something with. I forgot to ask Henrik when he was here to fetch Axel, but you're usually the one who takes care of the social calendar. By the way, Henrik is certainly slimmer. He must have lost a few kilos, eh?'

She sat up in bed again. It was suddenly hard to breathe.

'Hello?'

'Yes.'

'Are you still there?'

'Yes.'

'So what do you say to dinner on Sunday?'

Sunday? Dinner?

'I don't think we can make it. Listen, I have to run off to work now, I was just going out the door, I'll ring you in a day or two.'

She hung up and sat there holding the receiver to her ear. How could she have been so blind? So damned gullible. Like in a magnetic puzzle, all the bits suddenly fell into place. Late meetings. A sudden conference trip to Åland with lecturers she didn't know. Phonecalls abruptly terminated when she came in the door.

She got up, pulled on her robe, and went into the office. There had to be something. A note, a letter, a phone number.

She started with the desk drawers. Searched methodically through both sides, one drawer after another, half her mind determined, the other terrified of finding confirmation of what she really already knew.

Never in her life had she believed that she would ever end up in a situation like this. Never.

She found nothing. Only evidence of their family's validity. Life insurance policies, passports, bank statements, Axel's vaccination card, the key to the safe deposit box. She went on to the bookshelf. Where? Where would he hide something that she could never be allowed to find? Was there any single place in this house where she never looked? Where he knew that his secret would be safe?

Suddenly she heard the front door open.

Trapped like a thief she hurried out of the room and back to the bedroom. She had to think, had to find out. Who was she? Who was the other woman who was taking her husband from her? Destroying her life. The threat pulsed through her body.

Just as she heard his steps coming up the stairs, she opened the bedroom door and stepped out.

They stood eye to eye, two metres from each other.

An eternity between them.

He looked surprised when he saw her.

'Aren't you at work?'

He kept going, heading for his place at the kitchen table, the everyday sound of the chair legs scraping on the wooden floor. Then he grabbed the newspaper and she lost all self-control. Without hesitation she went over to him, tore the paper out of his hands, and flung it across the room. He stared at her.

'Are you crazy?'

He still had the coldness in his eyes. An indifference that was just as effective as a police barrier. She was no longer welcome. Armed with his secret he sat safely ensconced, shielded from her attacks, while she stood naked and unprotected, with no effective weapon to use.

Rage flooded through her. She wanted to strike, wound, crush. Do harm in return. Regain the balance. She hated the weakness he was creating inside her.

'I only want you to answer one question. How long has this been going on?'

She saw him swallow.

'What's that?'

He must have sensed the danger, because he no longer dared meet her gaze. That reassured her, almost made her smile. Slowly but surely she was regaining the upper hand. She was the one who had right on her side. He had lied and cheated and would have to answer for his betrayal, would be put to shame.

She sat down on the chair across from him.

'All right, maybe you have several going at once, but I was thinking of the woman you were talking to on the phone last night.'

He stood up, went over to the sink, and drank straight out of the tap. She restrained herself from showering him with all the words that were clamouring to come out. The best torture would be to sit quietly; the worst thing she could do to him would be to force him to speak.

He straightened up again and turned to her.

'It was just a friend.'

'I see. Anybody I know?'

'No.'

Short and to the point. He looked straight at her and it made her waver. For the first time in a long while he was looking her in the eye with a steady gaze. Where was he getting the strength, if not from the fact that he was unjustly accused?

'What's the friend's name then? And where did you meet her? Because I assume it's a she.'

'Does that make any difference?'

'Yes. If my husband has such a good friend that he can call her in the middle of the night and wants to talk when I'm in bed in the next room, then I'd like to know about it.'

She could see that he hesitated, taking an unwashed coffee cup from the counter and putting it in the dishwasher. Then he came back and sat down at the table.

Husband and wife, face to face across their familiar kitchen table.

A sudden calm.

It was now that they should talk. A businesslike pause in the hurricane that permitted them to approach each other, as if they were going to talk about some other couple. All the questions would finally be answered, all the lies admitted. Reality would be unveiled and the truth would stand there raw and naked. What would happen afterwards was like an unspoken agreement and unimportant right now.

As long as the truth was finally told.

'Her name is Maria.'

Maria.

'And where did you meet her?'

'She's a graphic designer at Widman's.'

'How long have you known her?'

He shrugged.

'Maybe six months.'

'Why haven't you told me about her?'

No reply.

'Why did you call her last night?'

'How do you know I did?'

'Does that really matter? You did call, didn't you?'

'Yes. I rang her up last night. She's . . .'

He broke off and shifted position on the chair, looking as if he would like nothing better than to get up and leave.

'I don't know. She's nice to talk to.'

'About what?'

'Everything.'

'About us?'

'Yes, that has probably come up.'

She felt sick again.

'So what did you say?'

'Well, I suppose I've told her the truth.'

'Which is?'

He took a deep breath, revealing his reluctance.

'I've said that we, well, that I, what the hell, she's nice to talk to, that's all. She's a fun girl.'

A fun girl.

We don't have fun any more.

Maria.

Her husband had called Maria from Widman's last night at one thirty in the morning. He had called and talked with Maria while she lay alone in the bedroom with her hopeless questions and her lacy underwear.

Bloody hell.

What had he said? Had he told her about the champagne she had bought and about the trip? The mere thought made her want to throw up. Somewhere there was a woman who knew more about their relationship than she did herself, who possessed information about her life that even she couldn't find out. She felt betrayed, abandoned. At a disadvantage to a woman she had never even seen.

Reality was encroaching. The pause was over.

'And how do you think that makes me feel? That you sit there telling her everything about me and our relationship?'

He glanced longingly at the door to his office, but she had no intention of letting him off the hook.

'Don't you understand what it feels like? If you think we have problems then I'm the one you ought to talk to, not her.'

A brief silence. Then the indifference in his gaze again.

'I have the right to talk to whoever I want, you have nothing to do with it.'

There was a stranger sitting across the table.

Maybe he had always been one. Maybe she had never really known him. She had merely lived in the same house with him for fifteen years but never knew who he actually was. She simply didn't understand his rage. Why couldn't he at least understand how bad he was making her feel? Or if he did, why didn't it matter to him? Why did he keep striking when she was already vanquished?

He got up, and now there was something new in his eyes. Maybe it was utter disgust that she saw.

'You're just jealous that I'm having fun.'

'Oh, is that what you think? Do you sleep with each other too?'

She had to know.

This time he snorted.

'No, what the hell do you think? Just because we like talking to each other and having fun. You can save your fucking fantasies for your fucking business strategies.'

He went to his office and slammed the door.

Two years ago they had replaced the glass in that door, working on it together.

Maria at Widman's. She's a really fun girl.

She saw that the geranium in the kitchen window needed watering, and she got up to fetch the watering can. And then she mustn't forget to pay that bill for Axel's swimming lessons.

She stood there holding the watering can and staring out the window. A van was parked in the neighbour's driveway, and two men were busy unloading a large assortment of well-packaged appliances. Boom or bust. How different things could be just a few metres away.

She took her handbag and went downstairs to the front door.

'I'm looking for Maria.'

She was standing outside amongst the trees in the park. Ringing from inside the house had felt impossible. The mere thought of standing amongst their things and hearing this woman's voice at the same time was inconceivable. She didn't really know why, but for some reason she felt a tremendous urge to hear her voice. This Maria at Widman's who knew things about her that she didn't even know. What had Henrik said? What had he told her? Somehow she had to regain her equilibrium, create her own advantage.

'You're looking for a Maria?'

'Yes, Maria.'

If you have several, then pick the one who's the

most fun and who likes to stick her nose into things that are none of her business.

'You must have the wrong number.'

'Isn't this Widman's Graphics?'

'Yes it is, but there's no Maria here.'

She hung up and stood there. The adrenaline was pumping through her body but had no means of release. What, there was no Maria?

In her confusion she went round the corner of the house and saw the van pull out from the neighbour's driveway. She went in the front door and continued into the bathroom, letting her clothes drop to the floor.

Why was he lying to her? Why did he say that he was talking to Maria at Widman's when she didn't exist? She couldn't really ask him, didn't want to admit she was snooping, for goodness' sake. She had no intention of giving him the satisfaction of knowing that she had stooped to something like that.

She found them behind the shower gel Axel had given her for her birthday. Mostly she was surprised at his carelessness. Or had they been left there intentionally, as an open declaration of war? Perhaps someone who was so much fun and so good to talk to wanted to consolidate her new territory, make a show of strength as she took over.

He was lying to her.

That pig was lying to her, and the contempt for his cowardice aroused a new impulse inside her. A feeling she had never experienced before.

You must not lie. Especially not to someone who trusted you, someone who for fifteen years had trusted you and believed that you were her closest friend.

And when the lie also threatened the other person's entire life, it was unforgivable.

And the thing you definitely shouldn't do, without deliberately planning it, was to leave her earrings behind your wife's eucalyptus shower gel.

He had stayed with Anna after Yvonne Palmgren left them in peace. The only time he left the room was when he used the microwave in the staff room to heat up his lunch. He wondered how many Gorby's pirogi and pizza slices he had eaten in the past two years, but hurried back in to Anna before his mind would force him to calculate the exact number.

Two months had passed, then three. His mother still stayed locked in her room. The compulsion controlled his whole life, but escaping from this mute punishment would just make everything worse. After those nine words, the silence continued. Each night he would hurry off to deliver his newspapers and then rush back home so that she wouldn't have to be alone. His father stayed away. Now and then, but not very regularly, a letter would arrive with a few thousand-krona notes to pay the bills for the heating oil and electricity. There weren't very many other expenses in the household. He took money for groceries from his own wages. The house belonged to her, she had inherited it from her aunt. The income from Pappa's job as a plumber had been all they needed to cover the costs in the family; his mother had never needed to go out and work. Her entire identity revolved around her role of wife to her husband and mother to her son.

It was a Tuesday when he discovered the classified ads, and it all started with a catastrophe.

Every night the same ritual. He would collect the bundle of newspapers down by the pizzeria. There were always a few extra copies, and before each night's delivery he counted the copies so he would only have to take with him the exact number he needed. It was the only way to be completely sure that he hadn't missed someone's letterbox. He could never be entirely certain, though; many days the worry had pursued him when he imagined that he had skipped one subscriber and delivered two papers to another.

First he would count out the sixty-two papers he needed directly from the bundle. Then he took out the plastic sheeting he kept in his backpack to protect the newspapers from getting wet. After that he piled them up in six stacks of ten. He placed number sixty-one and sixty-two directly in the pouch on his bike rack. When he had checked the stacks of ten four times, he was ready to put them in the pouch and get going. Always exactly the same route.

And then, on this particular Tuesday, the unforgivable happened.

He had one copy left over.

Someone had been missed out.

It was easy enough to check the letterboxes at the houses, but what if someone had already managed to collect their paper and it wasn't their box that had been skipped? And what about the ten flats in the building above the pizzeria that had slots in their doors? How would he be able to see whether it was one of them he had missed?

He felt the panic rising.

The leftover paper burned in his hands and he couldn't get rid of it. He stood there on the steps outside the front door when he came home, and he still had the newspaper in his hand.

Sandviken to Falun 68, Skövde to Sollefteå 696.

He had to read it. He had to read every single word in it to neutralise the mistake.

He sat down on the steps. It was just beginning to get light. The stone steps were cold, and as soon as he had finished the first page he was so cold he was shivering, but he had to keep reading. Each individual letter of every word had to be seen and respected by the eye of a reader. That was the only way.

It was on page 12 that he found it.

'Postman wanted for the Stockholm district.'

At first the words seemed much too implausible, but again and again his eyes came back to them, and after he had read them eight times they were finally transformed into a possibility.

He knew that he couldn't keep living at home. The only way to make her start to live again was for him to disappear. He was watching over her, but she didn't want him there.

He looked out over the garden. The once well-tended perennials in the flower beds lay withered on the ground, helplessly tangled up with weeds.

He was the one who was the weed.

I don't want you to live here any more.

On page 16 everything fell into place. He was meant to have one paper left over on precisely this day, something had seen to it that he would be the one who was forced to read it. For once the compulsion had been on his side.

'1 room w/o kitchen, Sthlm, for rent to reliable person – moving abroad.'

He sat for a long time on the steps that morning. Later he made the two phonecalls, and four days later he took the train down to Stockholm to go to the job interview. He was back the same evening; she didn't even notice he was gone. The following weeks were one long waiting period, but he knew that it was all pre-ordained. When the positive news arrived that he had got the job and the room, he took them both as a matter of course. Proud that he had dared.

He hesitated for a long time outside the closed bedroom door that evening before he finally knocked. She never told him to come in. At last he pressed down the door handle anyway and opened the door a crack. She was lying there reading. The blue shade was pulled down and the bed lamp was lit. She pulled the covers up to her chin as if she wanted to hide. As if an intruder had entered her room. The single mattress on the double bed frame that was twice the width was a reproach. She slept next to an empty space that always reminded her with the most blatant clarity of the degradation and betrayal they had caused her.

'I'm moving to Stockholm.'

She didn't reply, just turned off the bed lamp and turned over on her side with her back to him.

He stood there for a while, incapable of saying anything more. Then he backed out and closed the door.

The last thing he saw was a glimpse of her flow-ered robe.

Yvonne Palmgren arrived at one minute to two. Greeted him curtly and then went to sit down in the chair by the window again. She wasn't smiling this time. She examined him with a gaze so intense that he regretted agreeing to the first conversation. He took hold of Anna's hand. Here he was safe.

'I've made a few calls this morning.'

'All right.'

One of the four neon-coloured pens in her breast pocket was missing.

Three! Oh no!

He wondered whether she knew. Whether with her solid psychological training and penetrating gaze she could see straight in to his well-concealed hell. The three pens were a sign, a way to weaken him, a dec-laration of war from her side to prove her superiority.

He squeezed Anna's hand harder.

She opened the plastic folder. Read a few words and looked at him again.

'I want to talk about the accident itself.'

The sudden feeling of encroaching danger.

'I know that you stated that you have no recollec-tion of the accident, but I want us to try to piece together your memories. I have the police report here.'

The woman in the chair regarded their intertwined fingers.

'I understand that this seems like a lot of trouble. Perhaps you would rather we talked about it some-where else? We can go to my office if you like.'

'No.'

She sat in silence for a bit. Her eyes penetrating.

'I don't remember.'

'I see that's what it says on this paper, but the truth is that you've chosen not to remember. The brain functions to protect us from traumatic experiences, it chooses to repress things that are too painful to remember. That doesn't mean that you don't remember: everything is still inside. Sooner or later it will come to the surface and you will have to deal with it, no matter how painful it might be. And that's precisely what I want to help you do. Help you remember so that you can move on. It's a difficult and painful job you have ahead of you, but it is absolutely crucial. You will most likely feel angry during our conversation, but that's all right, as long as you let your anger out. I want you to direct it to me for the time being.'

Not in here! Never before had it ventured out when Anna was present and protecting him.

'Do you understand what I mean, Jonas? I'm here to help you, even if it doesn't feel that way. Anna is dying and you must accept that. And you must accept that it's not your fault, that you did the best you could. No one can ask any more of a person.'

Kalmar to Karesuando 1664, Karlskrona to Karlstad 460.

'All I know is what I read in the police report, and of course the hospital protocol when she was admitted. That she was struck by anischemic brain damage due to lack of oxygen. What's the last thing you remember?'

Landskrona to Ljungby 142. Help me, Anna. Stop it!

'You had gone down to Årstaviken to eat lunch. Can you remember what day that was?'

'No.'

'Try to remember what it looked like. The trees, did you meet anyone, did it smell a certain way?'

'I don't remember. How many times do I have to tell you that?'

'You went out on the pier at the Årstadal Boat Club.'

He had to put an end to this conversation. Had to get this woman out of the room.

Her voice droned on without mercy.

'Anna decided to go for a swim even though it was late September. Can you recall if you tried to stop her?'

She was blocking Anna's defence.

'You stood and waited on the pier. Can you recall how far out she swam before you realised she was in danger?'

Anna's head under water. Trelleborg to Mora. Damn. Not three. Eskilstuna to Rättvik 222.

The three neon pens on her large bosom were like a screeching reproach. The relentless voice that filled up every space inside him but mercilessly kept grinding away without noticing that he was about to explode.

'When she disappeared you swam out to try and help her. Another man came by and saw what was happening. He swam out to try and help the two of you, do you remember his name?'

'I don't remember!'

'His name was Bertil. Bertil Andersson. The man who helped you. The two of you managed to get her to the beach and Bertil Andersson ran to the boat club to ring for an ambulance. Try, Jonas, try to remember how it felt.'

He straightened up. He couldn't take any more.

'Don't you hear what I'm fucking saying, woman? I don't remember!'

She didn't take her eyes off him. Just sat calmly in her chair, watching him.

He found her in the attic. She had the flowered robe on and it was the evening before he was going to move away. His bags were already packed and waiting in the hallway. The ceiling was low and she hadn't needed a chair, only the low plastic stool that he had used as a child to reach the washbasin.

'How does it feel now?'

Her words drove him over the edge.

'Get out of here! Get out and leave us in peace!'

She remained sitting there. Didn't move from the spot, but kept on boring through him with her evil eyes. Calm and collected, firmly resolved to crush him.

'Why do you think you get so angry?'

Something burst inside him. He turned his head and looked at Anna.

She betrayed him. She lay there so innocent in her unconsciousness, but she had apparently not forgotten how to betray him. Once again she intended to leave him, alone. After all he had done for her.

Damn it.

He couldn't trust her even now. Even now she wouldn't do as he wished.

But he would show her. He wouldn't let her go.

Not this time either.

She decided to go to the day-care centre. A purely physical need to attempt to evade the threat she felt. Her world was starting to come crashing down. She felt petrified, robbed of every avenue of escape. Somewhere an unknown enemy was forging secret plans, and the one person she thought she could trust had proven to be allied with someone on the other side of the battle line. Had proven to be a traitor.

The signal from her mobile forced her to pull herself together. She saw from the display that it was from the day-care centre.

'Eva.'

'Hi, it's Kerstin from day-care. It's nothing serious, but Axel fell and hit himself on the slide and would like to be picked up. I tried to get hold of Henrik, who usually collects him, but he's not answering.'

'I'm on my way, I'll be there in fifteen minutes.'

'He's all right, he just got scared. Linda is sitting with him in the staff room.'

She hung up and set off in a hurry. The pavement on the old suburban street was broken up because they were installing remote heating and broadband, and she had to stop behind a queue of people as they let a car through.

Broadband.

Even faster.

She looked at the old turn-of-the-century houses lining the street. In this part of the neighbourhood they were big, like shrunken manor houses, not like at their end where the houses were smaller, starter opportunities for normal white-collar workers to have their own home.

A hundred years. How much had changed since then. Was there actually anything in society that was the same? Cars, aeroplanes, telephones, computers, the job market, gender roles, values, beliefs. A century of change. And it also encompassed the worst atrocities that humankind had ever devised. She had often compared her own life to how it must have been for her grandparents. So many things they had been forced to live through, learn, adapt to. Would any generation ever have to experience as much development and change as they had done? Everything changed. She could only think of one thing that was the same. Or was expected to be the same. Family and a lifelong marriage. It was supposed to function just as before, despite the fact that all external stresses and conditions were different. But marriage was no longer a common undertaking in which man and woman each took care of their own indispensable contributions. Mutual dependence was gone. Nowadays men and women were self-supporting units that were brought up to make it on their own, and the only reason they chose to get married was for love. She wondered if that was why it was so hard to make a marriage work, because the whole lifestyle depended on keeping love alive. And scarcely anyone in their child-bearing years had time to nourish it. Love was taken for granted and had to make it as best it could amongst all the things that required attention. And it seldom survived. More was needed for love to last. At least half of their friends had separated in recent years. Children who switched from one parent to the other every other week. Heart-rending divorces. She swallowed. The thought of other people's relationship problems was not making her own any easier to handle.

As daily life became more and more grey in recent years, she had thought a good deal about what was missing. And she wished that she had had someone to share her thoughts with. She had her girlfriends, of course, but lunch with the girls usually ended in general complaints about life. A statement more than a discussion about why life was the way it was. But one thing they all had in common. The weariness. The feeling of inadequacy. The lack of time. In spite of all the time-saving devices that had been invented since the houses along the street had been built, time was increasingly a rare commodity. Now they were putting in broadband to help save them even more precious seconds. Mail could be answered even more rapidly, decisions taken as soon as the alternatives arose, information retrieved in a second, information which then had to be interpreted and properly pigeonholed. But what about the human being in the background, whose brain was supposed to handle all this, what happened to her? As far as Eva knew, she had not undergone a product upgrade in the last hundred years.

She thought about the story she had heard about the group of Sioux Indians who during the 1950s were flown from their reservation in North Dakota to have a meeting with the President. With the help of jet engines they were whisked thousands of miles to the capital. When they entered the arrival hall at Washington airport, they sat down on the floor, and despite insistent appeals for them to go to the waiting limousines, they refused to get up. They sat there for a month. They were waiting for their souls, which could never have moved as fast as their bodies did with the help of the aeroplane. Not until thirty days later were they ready to meet the President.

Perhaps that was just what people should do, all the stressed-out people who were trying in vain to make their lives work. Sit down and wait to catch up. But weren't they already sitting there all together? Not exactly waiting for their souls, but they were all sitting in their own cosy living rooms, so that they could get completely involved in all the docu-soaps on their TV sets. Act shocked at the shortcomings of others and their inability to handle relationships. How did people cope, really? And then quickly change the channel to avoid taking a look at their own behaviour. So much easier to sit in judgement over others' behaviour from a distance.

She opened the door to Axel's section of the day-care centre and stepped inside, pulling on the light-blue plastic slippers and continuing towards the staff room. She saw them through the glass window in the door and stopped. He was sitting on Linda's lap eating a ginger snap. His hand was wrapped around a lock of her blonde hair and she was rocking him back and forth with her lips against his head.

The anger that had kept her going sank away and again opened up to the devastating powerlessness.

How could she ever protect him from everything that happened?

Don't cry here.

She swallowed, opened the door and went in.

'Look, here comes Mamma.'

Axel let go of Linda's hair and hopped down to the floor. Linda smiled to her, shyly as always. Eva made an effort to smile back and lifted Axel into her arms, as Linda got up and came over to them.

'He got a little bump there, but I don't think it's too serious. I told them not to go on the slide after it rained, it's so slippery then but . . . They probably forgot.'

'Feel, Mamma.'

She felt the little swelling on the back of his head. It was hardly noticeable and definitely nothing Linda should feel guilty about.

'It's nothing serious. It could have happened any-where.'

Linda smiled shyly again and went towards the door.

'We'll see you tomorrow then, Axel. Bye.'

They held each other's hand on the way home. When Axel had got over his anger at having to walk and not ride in the car as they usually did, he seemed to enjoy the walk.

A welcome respite.

He was the only one talking. She walked in silence and replied in monosyllables when necessary.

'And then when Ellinor took the ball we got mad and then Simon hit her on the leg with the stick but Linda said that you couldn't do that and then we couldn't play any more.'

He kicked at a pebble.

'Linda is really nice.'

'Yes.'

'Do you think Linda is nice too?'

'Yes, I do.'

'That's good, because Pappa does too.'

Yes. When he's not fucking someone in the shower at home.

'Of course he does.'

He kicked the pebble again, farther this time.

'Yes, he does, because one time when we were having a snack with her he gave her a big hug and they didn't know I saw.'

Everything stopped and turned white.

'What is it, Mamma? Aren't we going to walk any more?'

In a single instant everything turned upside down.

In a second the realisation erased every hint of trust, belief, confidence.

Linda!

It was Linda.

Everything she had believed and could count on had suddenly turned into yet another lie, another betrayal.

That woman, who had just been sitting so protectively with her lips against her son's skin, whom she had just reassured and told it wasn't serious, she was the one, she was the person who was trying to destroy their family. Like an amoeba she had wormed her way into their life and hidden her intentions behind her feigned concern.

Was there anything to hold on to? Anything she could trust to be as it should be?

How long had this been going on? Were there any others who knew about it? Maybe all the parents knew. Only she, poor Axel's jilted mamma, was left in the dark about whether her husband was having a secret affair with their child's day-care teacher.

The degradation was like a razor blade pressed against her wrist.

'Mamma, come on.'

She looked around, no longer conscious of where she was. The sound of a car approaching and slowing down. Jakob's mother rolled down the window.

'Hi, are you on your way home? You can ride with me if you want.'

Did she know something? Was she one of them who knew and gave her pitying looks behind her back?

'No.'

'Please, Mamma, can't we?'

'We're walking.'

Eva gave her a swift glance, took Axel's hand and pulled him along with her. Jakob's mother drove alongside.

'By the way, the parents' group has to have a meeting soon to plan that Stone-Age camp at the day-care. Do you have time this week?'

It was impossible to answer, there were no words. She quickened her steps. Five metres more to the path across the park. Without answering she turned and pushed Axel in front of her along the path. Behind her she heard the car idle and then drive off.

Linda. How old could she be? Twenty-seven, twenty-eight? She didn't have any children, Eva knew that at least. And now she had managed to seduce one of her day-care children's fathers without having the least idea of what it meant to be responsible for a life.

She looked at the little body in front of her. Colourful red PVC-coated trousers like balloons around his short legs. He started to run when he saw his house.

She stopped.

Axel took a short cut through the lilac hedge and vanished through the front door. Her son in the same house as the traitor. That cowardly shit who didn't even have the courage to admit his betrayal.

What he had done was unforgivable. She would never ever forgive him for it.

Never.

Ever.

For the first time in two years and five months he was going to spend the evening somewhere besides Karolinska Hospital. His anger at Anna's betrayal would not let him go, and by God he would show her. She could lie there all alone and wonder where he was. Tomorrow he would tell her that he had been at the pub having a good time. Then she'd regret it, realise that she could actually lose him. If she didn't shape up maybe he would do as they wanted. Let go and move on. Then she could lie there and rot and nobody would give a damn.

The psychotherapist monster had managed to convince him to agree to one more conversation. It had been the only way to get rid of her, which was absolutely necessary just then. Anna hadn't shown any remorse at all about her betrayal, and the growing compulsion had made him furious. But later he made her understand and it subsided again.

He had walked all the way into town. Drove home and parked the car on the street, and then began his walk without going inside the flat. Followed the path along Årsta Cove and then the old Skanstull Bridge towards Söder. In Götgatsbacken he passed one pub after another, but it only took one look through the big plate-glass windows to make him carry on. So many people. Even though it was a normal Thursday, people were jammed in everywhere and his courage failed him. He still wasn't ready to go in anywhere.

Later it was so obvious that he would keep on walking, passing by all the pubs in Söder, continuing north across the locks at Slussen and into Gamla Stan, the Old Town, as if his walk had been predetermined.

He was halfway across Järntorget, heading for Österlånggatan, when he caught sight of her.

A window with a red awning.

On a bar stool, gazing straight out through the window, she sat alone slowly twirling an almost empty beer glass. He stopped abruptly. Stood quite still and stared at her.

The resemblance was striking.

The high cheekbones, the lips. How was it possible for anyone to be so similar? He hadn't seen her eyes for a long time. Or the hands that never touched him.

So beautiful. So beautiful and utterly alive. Just like before.

He could feel the dull, heavy beats of his heart.

Suddenly she got up and moved farther back in the pub. He couldn't bear losing sight of her. He hurried the last few metres across the square and without hesitation opened the door and went inside. She was standing by the bar. All fear suddenly gone, only a firm resolve that he had to be near her, hear her voice, speak to her.

The far end of the bar made a ninety-degree turn, and that's where he sat so he could see her face. It almost made him stop breathing. There was almost an aura around her. All past longings, all beauty, all that was worthwhile gathered in this body, large as life before him.

Suddenly she turned her head and looked at him. He stopped breathing. Nothing could make him move his gaze from her eyes. She turned to the barman.

'A pear cider, please.'

The barman took down a glass from the rack above his head and served the cider. She had no ring on her left hand.

'That'll be forty-eight kronor.'

She made a move towards her handbag and he didn't hesitate an instant. Just let the words come as a matter of course.

'May I buy that for you?'

She turned her eyes towards him again. He saw that she was hesitant and waited breathlessly for her decision. If she said no he would be finished.

Then she gave him a faint smile.

'Certainly.'

Yet he wondered in confusion if it was actually joy he felt. He hadn't felt this way for so long that he couldn't identify the feeling. Only a certainty that everything was obvious, meant to be; there was nothing to be afraid of any more.

A complete, all-encompassing calm.

'Thank you,' he said.

How could he hide his gratitude? Relieved, he hurried to open his wallet.

'I'll have the same.'

He quickly put a hundred-krona bill on the bar and the barman gave him a glass. When he turned back to her she smiled at him.

'I'm the one who should be saying thanks,' she said.

He raised his glass to her and felt his smile spread through his whole body.

'No, that's not true, I should say it. Cheers, then.'

'Cheers.'

'And welcome.'

Their glasses met. The contact passed like a shock through his body. He looked at her over the rim of the glass, his eyes refusing to let go. He had to memorise every contour, every feature. Until the next time he saw her.

She drank again, two deep swallows. When she finished he would offer her another.

Again and again.

'My name is Jonas.'

She smiled, amused.

'There you see.'

Suddenly he was unsure. How could he get her to talk? Somehow he had to win her trust. Maybe she thought he had been too forward in buying her a cider.

'I don't usually buy cider for strange women, if that's what you think. But I wanted to buy one for you.'

She gave him a quick look and then stared down into her almost empty glass.

'Is that so? Why me in particular?'

He couldn't reply. How could she ever understand?

'What's your name?'

The question was so inadequate. He wanted to know everything. Everything she had ever thought, everything she had ever felt. An inner jubilation at even being able to think these things.

She paused before she answered, and he understood

her. He couldn't expect her to trust him. Not yet. But soon she would realise what he had understood as soon as he caught sight of her.

And as if she too was suddenly aware of the import of their meeting, she smiled at him again. A shy smile, as if she were telling him something in confidence.

'My name is Linda.'

Her first instinct had been to rush in and confront him with everything she knew. Shove the truth down his throat and tell him to go to hell. But in the next instant she realised that that was precisely what he wanted.

Go to hell.

Suddenly she grasped what he was trying to do. Standing in the park with their defiled home before her, it struck her like lightning out of a clear blue sky. She figured out his plan. All at once it was ridiculously obvious.

The cowardly swine was once again trying to push the responsibility onto her.

Once again he thought he could hide behind her capacity for action.

Instead of accepting the consequences for what he had done and for once making his own decision, he thought he could force her to leave *him*. Get rid of the guilt so that for all his days he would be able to hide behind the fact that it was her decision; she was the one who wanted a divorce, she was the one who was leaving.

She wasn't going to make it that easy for him. Not at all.

She felt a stubborn contempt.

He couldn't even manage his own infidelity without her.

Her decisiveness filled her with a liberating calm. She was in control again. Finally she knew what she should do.

She needed confirmation of just one thing to be able to hold out.

Just one thing.

She hadn't said a word before she left. Henrik and Axel were playing a computer game and had closed the door to the office; he'd notice she was gone soon enough. She was more than pleased not to see him. She still wasn't sure that she could manage to conceal her hatred, but she had the whole night to summon her strength. Tomorrow he would have his faithful wife back; but first she had to get someone to confirm that she was good enough.

She looked out over Järntorget. She had stopped briefly on the way into Gamla Stan to have a well-deserved pick-me-up. It was a long time since she'd been out on the town at all, and she couldn't remember ever going out alone before. Always having to rush home with a guilty conscience. At work because she wasn't at home, and at home because she couldn't manage to do her job properly.

She took the last gulp from her glass and turned around. This was definitely the wrong place for her plans. Couples eating dinner and groups that didn't want to include anyone else. No, one more cider and then she'd get going.

She went up to the bar.

She heard the door open behind her. The barman stood with his back turned, filling bowls with peanuts. She turned her head and glanced at the man who had just come in. Now he was standing right in front of her at the short end of the bar.

Way too young.

The barman came over to her.

'A pear cider, please.'

He ducked down and stood up again with a bottle in his hand. With his other hand he reached for a glass from the rack above their heads.

'That'll be forty-eight kronor.'

She already had her hand around her purse in her handbag. And then came the surprising question.

'May I buy that for you?'

At first she didn't realise that he was talking to her. Surprised, she looked at the man standing at the bar nearby. Maybe twenty-six, twenty-seven, grey jacket, blond hair combed back, looked pretty good.

Why not?

'Certainly.'

For a second she thought he might be kidding, because he just stood there smiling at her. Then he took his wallet out of an inside pocket.

'Thank you. I'll have the same.'

He placed a hundred-krona note on the bar and the barman took down another glass. She was smiling to herself. He had to be more than ten years younger than her, so she obviously had a little sex appeal left.

She wondered what they were doing at home. Whether Axel had gone to bed. She pushed away the thought and tried to smile.

'I'm the one who should be saying thanks.'

He raised his glass to her.

'No, that's not true, I should say it. Cheers, then.'

'Cheers.'

'And welcome.'

There was something about his eyes. His gaze was so penetrating that she was almost embarrassed. As if he were looking right into her, could read all her thoughts, and she had no intention of sharing them with anyone. For an instant she regretted letting him buy her a drink. Now she would have to stay here, and she had other plans for the evening. The faster she finished her drink the better. She took two deep swallows.

'My name is Jonas.'

She drank a bit more. All her thoughts were occupied with the hatred she felt. She couldn't sit here chatting as if everything were normal.

'There you see.'

Soon she had finished the drink.

'I don't usually buy cider for strange women, if that's what you think. But I wanted to buy one for you.'

'Is that so? Why me in particular?'

He stood looking at her in silence.

'What's your name?'

He gave her that smile again. Utterly disarming. And then those eyes that went right through her, as if he really wanted to see into her. But her hatred was her own, he mustn't see it, no one could see it. If anyone should see her shameful hatred, it would make her weak. She had to learn to act normal, otherwise she would never be able to carry out her plan.

She took another swallow.

Good Lord, he had to be at least ten years younger than she was. Quite harmless. He would be good to practise on. For a while he had made her forget that she was the one in control. His undisguised interest had made her uncertain, but that was actually her goal for the evening. He was standing right in front of her and offering her everything she had come here to find. She suddenly regarded him with new interest. He wanted her even though she was at least ten years older. Could she ask for better proof?

She smiled again.

'My name is Linda.'

She was astounded to hear her own lie. And how easy it was to deliver it. Actually it wasn't even a lie. It wasn't talented Eva who was standing at the bar, it was some other woman. A woman who had put aside everything she believed in and without the slightest pang of conscience was scheming to achieve her goal and take what she wanted even if it actually belonged to someone else.

To a Linda.

'Hi, Linda. Would you like another cider?'

She saw to her dismay that the glass was empty. In the next moment she was aware of her intoxication. Everything suddenly far away, only the moment was present. A restful moment in which nothing really mattered very much. Nothing to gain, nothing to lose. She had the whole night ahead of her.

'Sure. Why not?'

He looked pleased and called over the barman.

'Can we get another round?'

She got her glass and they sat on their bar stools, he with his knees touching her and she with her arms resting on the bar. The barman changed the tape and took a few dance steps when the intro to an old Earth, Wind and Fire song poured out of the loudspeakers. She couldn't remember what it was called. But they used to play it at parties in high school.

They sat in silence for a while. She wasn't sure that she felt like staying, but she should at least give him a chance. He was just as good as any other man. She took another sip of cider and looked around. More patrons had arrived. A group of middle-aged Englishmen came in the door. In the mirror behind the bar she could see between the bottles that the man named Jonas was still watching her.

'May I pay you a compliment?'

She turned her head and met his intense gaze. It made her want to stay and enjoy his unfeigned admiration.

'Sure, be my guest.'

'This might sound silly, but I think I'll say it anyway.'

Suddenly he seemed embarrassed and glanced away for a few seconds before he looked at her again.

'Do you know that you're the only person in here who looks really alive?'

She laughed and took another sip.

'Oh no, that's a good one. I haven't heard that one before.'

He was serious now. Just sat silently and looked at her.

She waved her hand in an attempt to make light of his seriousness.

'I think they all look fairly alive. They're moving, at least.'

A hint of irritation. A crease between his dark eye-brows.

'You can make a joke about it if you like, but I meant what I said. It was intended as a compliment. You have a kind of sad look in your eyes, but it's obvious that you have a heart that really knows how to love.'

His words pierced the soothing calm.

A heart that really knows how to love. Ha!

Her heart was as black as a windowless cellar. No love would ever be able to survive in there any more. But right now she was sitting in a bar in Gamla Stan, she and this Jonas who talked like a bad poet and was ten years younger but who looked at her with a desire that she couldn't recall ever experiencing. She felt a sudden longing that he would touch her, lose control and let loose all the desire she could see in his eyes. Prove that he couldn't resist her. That she was worth loving.

The alcohol gave her the courage she needed.

She turned towards him and met his eyes before she placed her hand over his on the bar.

'Is it far to your place?'

He lay utterly still, couldn't move, as if split in two. One half filled with a satisfaction and an anticipation that he didn't think it was possible to feel. Everything he had ever dreamed of.

Ten hours earlier he hadn't even known that she existed and, now, in the short time he had known her, she had given him everything he could ever have desired. Trembling she had given herself to him, offered him her most sensitive places. The trust she showed had opened his mind wide, all was tenderness, an explosion when the loneliness cracked open.

And then the calm she created. Her confident hands over his skin covered him with a protective layer, purified him, set him free. All the desire that had so long chafed inside him had burst out and flowed into her. The emptiness was gone.

But then the devastating knowledge that he had no right to feel this way.

The other half contained the guilt.

Now it was proven. In a swift descent he had become a deceiver and a cheat. He had let Anna lie alone while he gave himself to another woman. Poured out all the desire he had been saving so long for her. That she should have received.

He was no better than his father.

*   *   *

She was gone when he woke up. Only a brown hair on the pillow proved that she had really been there. The hair, and the sated hunger of his skin.

They hadn't said a word to each other. Their hands and bodies had told all they needed to know.

He sat up and was aware of the cold in the room. He had forgotten to turn on the heater when they came home. He wondered if she had felt cold. He turned the thermostat all the way up in the living room and the kitchen and went into the bathroom. The light was on and the blue-edged hand towel was tossed on the floor. He felt a slight pang of distaste but it couldn't reach him. Her touch lay like a shield around him, an impenetrable armour, it couldn't reach him any longer.

He hung up the towel and turned on the water in the bathtub, waited until it was half full and then climbed in. The hot water reminded him of her hands and he could feel his desire rise again. So many years he had forbidden himself to give in. Now he could no longer resist the urge, not even now after she had just left. What had she succeeded in waking inside him?

He sat down and leaned back. The memory of her nakedness was like a lifelong gift. He could see her before him. How she had closed her eyes and abandoned herself to the pleasure he could give her.

Her hands. Her lips. The taste of her. Her skin against his, united, no beginning, no end.

How could he have resisted her? She was everything he dreamed of. A vibrant woman who wanted to have him, take hold of him, love him. Made him reach a pleasure he didn't think was possible. What terrible god could possibly demand that he say no?

He got up, climbed out of the bathtub and dried himself with the blue-edged hand towel. The one she must have just used. Suddenly he felt like crying. How could he touch Anna now that his hands were full to the brim with another woman?

With Linda.

He hardly dared think of her name. Anna would discover what had happened. She would feel the betrayal, that he hadn't managed to keep his promise.

And what would he say when Linda called? She hadn't asked for his phone number, but she knew where he lived. He was here in the bathroom, but all his desire was with her.

He sat down on the toilet seat and put his head in his hands.

No matter what he did, he would have to betray one of them.

He had to go to the hospital. Right now, he had to drive over to see Anna and confess what he had done. He had to win her forgiveness. Without it he could not survive.

The telephone rang. He looked at his watch. Ten past seven. Naked he went back into the living room. It must be her. Who else would call this early? She must have called enquiries to get his phone number. What should he say? And how could he resist answering and hearing her voice?

The most fantastic thing was that he could answer after five rings. It couldn't affect him any more. His whole body smiled with this realisation when he picked up the receiver and answered.

'Hi, this is Jonas.'

'Jonas, this is Björn Sahlstedt at Karolinska Hospital. It's probably best if you come over. Right away.'

When she came out the front door of the building it was ten after four in the morning, and she didn't know where she was. The taxi had driven south from Gamla Stan and took a right at Gullmarsplan, she remembered that, but then she had lost her bearings. She turned around. To the right of the entrance hall she had just come out of there was a street sign on the wall, and she took a few steps closer so she could read it in the dark. Storsjövägen. She was in a dead end, and she started walking down the street. The façades of the buildings were dark with shiny black windowpanes. Only a few lights were on.

She was grateful that he didn't wake up when she got out of bed. For about an hour she lay still, pretending she was asleep, until his regular breathing assured her that he was sleeping. Only then did she dare open her eyes. A bed-sit, strangely empty of objects. Maybe he was just living there temporarily. Only the walls belied this idea. A great number of oil paintings of various sizes, all with colourful abstract patterns, covered almost every square centimetre.

He had fallen asleep with his lips against her left shoulder. It was noticeably cold in the flat. Carefully, so that he wouldn't wake up, she drew away from him, got up and rummaged on the floor for her clothes.

In his bathroom mirror she saw a woman who was a stranger. A woman who had seduced a twenty-five-year-old, gone home with him to his flat and to bed. She still could not decide whether it had had the effect on her that she had imagined.

Everything seemed shut down inside her.

On the way up the stairs to his flat she became nervous. The courage of intoxication had vanished and for a moment she wanted to leave. But then she envisaged Henrik and Linda together and it made her feet continue through the door of the flat. As soon as she entered the hallway she pressed herself against him, just to conceal her inner imbalance, and his desire was so strong that they scarcely managed to get their clothes off. His frantic hands had fumbled over her body, and it occurred to her that perhaps he was a virgin, but she did her best to instil self-confidence in him, pretending to enjoy his clumsy attempts.

The street ended at an intersection, and she took out her mobile and rang for a taxi.

His name was Jonas and Hansson was the name on his door. That was all she knew, and she had no interest in knowing more. He had done his part and she had done hers.

It was like a void inside her, an inability to be touched. The only man who had touched her in fifteen years was Henrik, and now she had given herself to a total stranger.

And she couldn't care less.

There was a light on in the entrance hall when she

came home. She took out her purse, took out her wedding ring and slipped it back on her finger. As quietly as she could she hung up her coat and went into the kitchen. Everything was quiet. Axel's plate was still on the table, and she could see that they had eaten spaghetti with meat sauce. A completely normal dinner. Henrik's mobile lay on the kitchen counter. Not a single message. The call list showed no numbers, either received or called; it must have been erased. He thought he was smart, that bastard.

She went into Axel's room. The moon-shaped night-light was on and the floor was covered with toys, but the bed was empty as usual. She sat down on the floor. An Action Man lay next to her on the carpet, with arms and legs stiffly extended. It lay there abandoned by his defenceless little hands – powerless to stop his life coming apart.

She looked at the toy she was holding in her hands. Who had given him this? The right hand was shaped to grip its weapons.

She stood up quickly. Henrik's keyring was in his jacket pocket and she continued down to the cellar. The gun cabinet. Where he kept his hunting rifles. The only place in the house where she never went.

She found them under a red box of ammunition: a bundle of computer-printed letters with no envelopes. She only managed to read the first four lines. Pressure gripped her chest. She leafed rapidly through them and found at the bottom of the pile two folded lists from the Swedish Real Estate Agency. Properties T 22 and K 18. That bastard was looking for a new place to live, well aware that she could never afford to keep living in the house without him. He didn't even have the courtesy to tell her that she would soon be forced to move out of her home.

Never in her life had she thought that anyone would treat her this way.

For the time being she couldn't do anything to Henrik.

Linda, on the other hand, had no idea what was in store for her.

He ended up in the middle of rush-hour traffic. It usually took him eighteen minutes to drive to Karolinska, sometimes up to twenty-four, but this morning he made it only as far as the Bromma turn-off in the usual amount of time. He kept changing lanes, heading for Essinge, but that didn't help either.

Dr Sahlstedt had said that it was probably best if he came at once.

But why hadn't he told him to hurry?

Near Tomteboda there was a three-car pile-up, and after he managed to squeeze past the accident the traffic eased a bit. So many times he had driven this way. He wondered how many. And then the relief, despite his worry, that nobody was forcing him to count.

She had healed him.

And then the next thought. Forgive me, Anna. Forgive me.

The smell of fried bacon. It would forever be associated with that afternoon when she left him. He sensed the danger as soon as he came into the hall. It wasn't only the smell of frying, there was something else in the air as well. The car had been parked in the driveway, so his father was home, and at this time of day his mother was always home too. He stood quite still with his coat on and wondered if anyone had heard him come in.

Not a sound to be heard. And yet he knew that they were there.

He stretched out his hands in front of him, but couldn't make himself touch the jacket he was supposed to take off. He felt the compulsion growing stronger and headed for the bathroom to wash his hands.

'Jonas!'

He stopped in mid-stride. It was his father shouting.

'Yes?'

'Come here.'

He swallowed.

'I just have to wash my hands.'

'Stop that foolishness right now and come here, I say!'

He had been drinking. And he was angry. He almost always was when he was drunk, but he usually only got drunk on weekends. Then you had to watch out, never knowing when he would explode. Or why.

The compulsion retreated. The fear of what was waiting out there in the kitchen took over instead. He pulled off his jacket and placed it on a chair. Everything was quiet again. Quietly he went towards the kitchen.

She was sitting at the table.

He stood leaning against the counter with a glass in his hand. Funny how water and alcohol could look so much alike.

On the kitchen table in front of her lay a man's white shirt.

She turned her head and looked at him when he

came in, and the expression on her face filled him with terror. He wanted to run to her and hold her, comfort her, protect her. Lay his head on her lap like he had done when he was little and she would stroke his hair and say that everything was going to be all right. So many times they had sought comfort in each other, united against his father's unpredictable weekend rages.

He looked at his father. He had those eyes he got when he had been drinking. When you knew he was someone nobody knew.

He took a swig from his glass.

'Mamma has found a shirt with a little lipstick on it. That's why she's so mad.'

She had found out. In the midst of all the commotion over her reaction the words filled him with relief. Finally his father had been forced to confess. Now he would be free of his responsibility to protect her, be spared all the circumlocutions and lies that had come between them. Finally he would be hers again, totally, could stand on her side. As he had always done.

His father slammed down his glass on the counter and turned to his mother sitting at the kitchen table with her back to him.

'What should I do, do you think? Eh? You never contribute anything! Just roam around here at home looking like a goddamn dishrag and complaining that there's never enough money, that we never go on holiday or can afford anything. You'll just have to go out and get a job yourself then, if it's not enough!'

Jonas looked at his mother again and now he dared go over to her. He put his hand on her shoulder and she took it in hers.

Then he looked at his father. You bastard! We don't need you any more. We never did.

He could see the change in his father's eyes, which now belonged to a stranger. In the next instant his glass smashed against the tile above the cooker on the far wall.

'And you, you sanctimonious little bastard. Standing there comforting her like you never knew a thing.'

A few seconds passed, then his mother let go of his hand.

'If you only knew what he's been doing so that you wouldn't find out. He lies better than a con man, I don't know where he comes up with it all. But he gets it from you, I can see, your family has always been a pack of liars.'

His father continued without mercy.

'Why don't you tell her now? Tell her what a stud I am. How all the women except for her will do anything so I'll screw them. The one with the lipstick you've even met. So you saw it all for yourself.'

Two weeks later. He had been allowed to go along to the docks at Söderhamn. Was offered a chance to make a little extra money by helping out with a clean-up after a construction job where his father laid pipes. He was glad when they left, glad that they were going to spend two days together. Maybe he'd have a chance to talk to his father about how he felt, how he couldn't lie any more. He waited all day for an opportunity that never came. Then he thought: tonight when we eat dinner at the hotel, then I'll get my chance. She was already sitting in the dining room when they arrived, and before they even got their food his father had invited her over to their table. He ordered more and more beers. Jonas sat silently in shame at his father's increasingly ridiculous behaviour. About an hour later he gave Jonas a few hundred-krona notes and sent him out on the town. He didn't dare come back until around three in the morning. He needed to sleep. He was dead tired from the day's work, and the next morning they had to get up at six thirty and go back. She was still there in the hotel room. Their clothes lay scattered on the floor, her fat right leg was sticking out from the covers, and neither of them noticed him come in. He spent the rest of the night on a sofa in the lobby, but something inside him had finally had enough. In the morning he couldn't control all his pent-up rage any longer. For the first time he dared to refuse, and his father sat hungover in his underwear on the edge of the messy double bed and tried to beg for forgiveness. But Jonas was unyielding. This time he was going to tell him. He didn't intend to lie any more. When his father recognised the firmness in his threat he collapsed with his face in his hands, and with his gut hanging over the edge of his shorts he sobbed and begged him not to do it.

And Jonas had once more been forced into betrayal.

His mother turned her head and looked at him. She didn't say a word, but the question was crystal clear in her eyes. He lowered his eyes, couldn't look at her. He squatted down beside her, lowered his head, his face close to her right leg. He prayed to God that she would touch him. Show him with a single sign that she forgave him. That she understood that he never wished her any harm. That he did it all for her sake.

'Forgive me.'

A few seconds passed, maybe it was more.

Then she pushed the chair back and stood up. Without looking at either of them she left the kitchen.

And somewhere deep inside he already knew that she would never ever come back.

He parked the car right outside the main entrance of Karolinska in a no parking zone. If anyone gave him a parking ticket this time they would have themselves to blame.

The lift up to Anna's ward had never moved so slowly. On every floor there was someone who had to get on or off, and the stress he felt gave him a taste of lead in his mouth.

The corridor was empty. He hurried to Anna's door and had just put his hand on the door handle.

'Jonas, wait!'

He turned towards the voice. A nurse he had only seen a few times before came rushing towards him.

'Doctor Sahlstedt is coming. I think you should wait.'

He'd rather rot in hell. Nobody in the world could prevent him from going in to see her, he was going in this very instant.

He pulled open the door.

The bed was not visible from the doorway, but what he saw was enough.

A sudden inertia prevented him from entering the room. A passive moment, nothing that needed to be thought, done or felt.

A pause before everything would become clear.

He had an intense urge to close the door again, wishing he hadn't seen that the room was illuminated by a candle fluttering in the gust of air from the door he had just opened, sending its light flickering across the wall.

A hand on his shoulder cut off all possibility of escape and brought him back to what the future held. He turned his head and looked into Dr Sahlstedt's sad face. The unwelcome touch of the doctor's hand forced him forward and the next instant he saw her.

The room clean and tidy. Only the bed with Anna, the white sheets tucked in. The probes and tubes gone and all the machines rolled out to patients who still needed them.

Dr Sahlstedt went over to her.

'She had an embolism around four o'clock.'

Around four o'clock.

When he had been lying with his lips against Linda's skin.

'There was nothing we could do.'

He had lain there naked with all the desire he had saved up for Anna and himself given away to another woman.

He went over and sank down on the edge of the bed but couldn't bring himself to touch her. His hands were incontrovertible proof.

'Shall I leave you alone for a moment?'

He didn't answer, but he heard Dr Sahlstedt's steps cross the floor and the door shut.

Her hands crossed on her breast. The claw-like left hand trying to clutch the other. On her throat a white compress over the hole left by the respirator tube.

*   *   *

For a single evening he had left her alone, and then she seized her chance. She must have understood. Somehow she must have known that he was with another woman, and this was her punishment. For two years and five months she had lain here biding her time, waiting for the right moment when her revenge would hit him hardest. She had left him, once and for all, and she had chosen the moment with care.

He would never be forgiven. Her punishment was to never forgive him. The rest of his life he would have to live with the knowledge that she never ever forgave him for what he did.

He stood up and looked at the body in the bed. So much time he had spent winning her love. And all he had in return was her betrayal.

He could swear that he saw a smile on her lips. She lay there thinking that she had won, that she got her revenge. As if all he had done for her was not enough to absolve the guilt.

'I don't need you. Do you hear that, you whore? I've met a real woman, a woman who loves me for who I am and not like you ... like you ... who can only feel love as a game, as something to amuse oneself with as long as there's nothing more interesting going on.'

The sudden rage he felt surged through him and he spat out the words. He had to get her to react, make her understand that she had no more power over him, that she had not succeeded.

The door opened behind him and he turned around. Dr Sahlstedt came back, this time accompanied by the Monster Psychotherapist. They stopped abruptly inside the doorway and looked at him expectantly.

'How are you doing?'

It was the woman with the piercing eyes who was speaking to him. She had on the same red jumper and stupid plastic necklace as the day before. The three neon pens in her breast pocket left him completely unmoved.

He smiled at her.

'Let me tell you something. That necklace you're wearing. You know, it's probably the ugliest fucking necklace I've ever seen.'

Dr Sahlstedt stared at him. Yvonne Palmgren wasn't so easily startled. She took a couple of steps to the foot of the bed.

'I'm sorry for your loss.'

He smiled again.

'Are you?'

He turned to the bed table and blew out the candle.

'She does have a brother somewhere in Australia, but I don't know how much grief he's going to feel. So far, at least, he hasn't made an appearance. I don't know of anyone else who will care.'

Dr Sahlstedt came over to him and again placed an unwelcome hand on his shoulder.

'Jonas. We know that this comes as a shock for you but . . .'

He took a step back to avoid the doctor's touch.

'You can do what you like with the body. She has nothing to do with me any longer.'

The other two in the room exchanged a brief glance.

'Jonas, we have to . . .'

'I don't have to do anything. You wanted me to let go and move on. Well, that's what I'm doing.'

Without looking at the body in the bed he threw out his hand in their direction.

'Do whatever the hell you like.'

He went towards the door. He felt like he was floating. As if his feet weren't really touching the plastic mat they were walking on.

'Jonas! Wait a minute!'

They couldn't stop him. Nothing could stop him. He was going to get out of here and never come back. He was going to eradicate the memory of all the minutes, hours, days he had wasted in his all-consuming yearning.

Outside, life was waiting.

The only thing she had achieved with her ingenious revenge was to give him back his freedom. The guilt was under control.

An eye for an eye, a tooth for a tooth.

One betrayal paid back with another.

He was free.

Now he was all Hers.

All he had to do now was go home and wait for Her to call.

Maybe she had slept for an hour or so when the clock radio went on, she didn't know. She had spent the hours of dawn in a half-slumber, something inside her prevented her from sleeping properly, she had to be on guard. Asleep she was defenceless.

She reached out her arm and put off the alarm, got up and pulled on her robe. He lay there on the other side of the double bed, motionless and with his eyes closed; whether he was asleep or not it was impossible to tell. The distaste she felt made her wide awake. All feelings directed inward, in towards the dark. The fatigue could not reach her.

Nothing could reach her.

She leaned forward and slid her hands under Axel's sleeping body. She carefully lifted him up, carried him from the room and pushed the bedroom door shut.

She sank down in the sofa in the living room and looked at his sleeping face. So innocent, so completely free of guilt. She closed her eyes and forced back the pain prompted by his closeness. He was the only one who made her feel vulnerable, and there was no room for weakness now. In some way she had to defend herself against the feelings he awakened in her. Shield herself. If she allowed herself to give in she was lost, a victim, poor Axel's rejected mamma who had lost control over her life. Sometime in the future he would understand that she did it all for his sake. That she was the one who took responsibility and tried to protect him, not like his father.

'Axel, you have to wake up now. It's time to go to day-care.'

They arrived a bit late, just as she had planned. The children were already sitting on the floor in the play-room waiting for the session, and all the parents had hurried off to their jobs. Axel hung his jacket on the hook and at the same moment Linda came in from the kitchen with the fruit bowl in her hands.

'Hi, Axel.'

'Hi.'

A quick smile in her direction and then her gaze on Axel again.

'Come on, Axel, let's go in. The session is starting soon.'

There was a calm about her. The hatred felt almost enjoyable. All her energy was focused and she herself was without guilt. None of this ever had to happen, they were the ones who were forcing her. It was odd how a couple of unfamiliar earrings in one's shower could sharpen the senses.

Her words sharpened to spear tips.

'Oh Linda, have you got a moment? There's something I have to say.'

She could see a glint of fear in the other woman's eyes and was enjoying her power.

'Yes, of course. Axel, go in and sit down, then I'll come in and we can wave out the window.'

He did as she said. Maybe he could sense her

resolve. He vanished into the playroom and she turned back to Linda, looked at her for a while, conscious of the nervousness her silence was creating. Linda stood perfectly still. Only the fruit bowl in her hands was shaking.

'Well, it's like this . . . it's a bit difficult to talk about but . . . I still wanted to do it for Axel's sake.'

She fell silent again, resting in her advantage.

'It's just that . . . we're having a few problems at home right now, Henrik and I, and I thought it would be good if you heard about it, with regard to Axel, I mean. I don't know how aware he is but . . . in any case I do know how much he relies on you here at day-care, and it will probably be even more important for a while until we've managed to sort all this out.'

Linda's eyes searched the room in the hope of finding something to fix her gaze on.

'I see.'

I see? Weren't you the one who was so damned fantastic to talk with?

'I just wanted to tell you this, for Axel's sake.'

'Sure. Naturally.'

They stood motionless. It was clear that Linda wanted nothing more than to be allowed to leave. Maybe this was how they found each other. Realised that they shared the same improbable cowardice, always wanting to flee from anything that could be considered a real conversation.

Eva held her fast with her gaze.

'What a nice jumper you're wearing, by the way.'

Linda looked down at her jumper as if she had never seen it before.

'Thanks.'

Yes, little Linda. Now you've got a little something to wonder about.

'Will you tell Axel that I'll wave to him in the window?'

'Of course.'

'And thanks for listening.'

She smiled and put her hand confidingly on Linda's forearm.

'It feels so good to be able to tell you this. I'm sure that everything will work out. Every marriage has its ups and downs from time to time.'

She smiled, and maybe that's what Linda was trying to do as well.

'We'll come to get him at four as usual.'

She kept her hand on Linda's arm a moment too long before she turned to go.

He still wasn't awake when she got home. The door to the bedroom was closed, and she continued into the kitchen and put on some coffee. She had called in to work from her mobile. It was a serious flu she had come down with, and the doctor had given her a sick note, so it was probably best if Håkan took over her project for a while.

She took out the guest bed with the fold-down legs that had been a wedding present from Cissi and Janne. It was still in its original box and had barely been used.

Never before had an idea been so clear, so pure, so utterly free of hesitation and doubt. There was only a single driving force, and it was so powerful that it shoved everything else aside, justified every step she took, every thought.

One step at a time. It was the here and now that mattered. The future that she wanted no longer existed, he had taken it away from her.

Now she just had to see to it that he lost the future he wanted too.

And he wouldn't even know what hit him.

She finished making up the guest bed and stopped outside the bedroom door. She tried to smile a few times to practice her expression, but she mustn't overdo it. She had to try to behave like the Eva he thought he knew, the one who existed twenty hours ago, or else he would be suspicious.

She pressed down the handle with her arm and pushed open the door with her foot. He was awake and raised himself up on his elbow.

'Good morning.'

He didn't reply.

Didn't you hear me say good morning, you fucking pig?

He lay silent, staring at her as if it were a sharp axe and not a tray she held in her hands.

'What's that?'

She took a step into the room.

'It's called breakfast in bed.'

She was at his side and resisted the temptation to dump the hot coffee in his face. He sat up and she carefully set the tray over his legs.

'You don't have to worry, I don't intend to seduce you. I just want to talk a little.'

She smiled into the darkness, well aware that this was an even greater threat.

Then she sat down at the foot of the bed, as far

from him as she could get without leaving the room.

He sat quite still, pinned down by the tray straddling his legs.

'As you may have noticed, I wasn't home last night.'

'No. It would have been nice if you'd said something before you left.'

She swallowed. She couldn't let herself be provoked. The new Eva was a good, fine person who understood that he must have been worried.

'I know, that was stupid. I apologise, but I had to get out of here for a while.'

He didn't give in, but made use of the occasion to share some of his guilty conscience.

'Axel was sad and wondered where you were.'

She clenched her fist and concentrated on the pain her nails caused as they dug into her palm.

If you want to talk about guilt, then let's do that. Who causes him the most harm.

'I was out walking all night.'

She dropped her gaze and stroked her hand across the blue-checked sheet.

'I was thinking about everything that's happened here at home recently, how we're not getting along, how we act towards each other. I realise that it's just as much my fault that it's turned out like this.'

She looked up at him but had a hard time reading his reaction. His face was blank. He had been ready for strife and conflict and clearly didn't know how to act when she lay prostrate at his feet.

She smiled into the darkness again.

'I'd like to apologise for getting so angry about that thing about Maria at Widman's. Just to clear the air a bit, I realise that it's great that you have her to talk to, that it might actually be a good thing for us. If she's as smart as you say she is, she can probably help us get through all this.'

His expression made her lower her eyes again. She turned her head so that he wouldn't notice her smile and then kept talking with her face turned away.

'I know that you've been feeling bad for a while, and you said yourself that you don't think it's fun any more.'

She looked at him again.

'Why don't you go away for a little while? Think about how you want things to be, what it is you want. I'll take care of everything at home in the meantime, it's completely OK. The main thing is that you feel good again.'

He sat utterly still.

Well, Henrik, now it's a little harder, isn't it?

She stood up.

'I just want you to know that I'm here for you if you need me, I always have been even if I might not have been good at showing it sometimes. I'll do my best to try and improve. I'm here, and I always will be.'

Now he looked almost sick. His thighs were pressed against the underside of the tray and some of the coffee in the cup sloshed over the edge and ran under the plate of sandwiches.

She was amazed that she ever could have touched him. He sat there looking so pitiful and timid that she wanted to hit him.

Get up damn you, and stand up for yourself!

She backed towards the door. She had to get out of the room before she lost control.

The last thing she saw was how he lifted the tray aside. She left the bedroom, continued downstairs and went straight to the gun cabinet.

There was no parking ticket on his car when he came out. It didn't surprise him much, he only noted it as something natural. For the last time the main doors had slid aside when they sensed his presence, but this time they hadn't tossed him out into fear and loneliness, longing for the next time he would be allowed inside. This time they had slid aside deferentially and wished him well in his new life.

Now it would all begin. Everything he had gone through up till now had been a test of whether he deserved what now awaited him. He could forgive life for the injustice after injustice. Together with her everything would be repaid.

For the last time he turned on to Solnavägen and took a right towards Essingeleden. The rush-hour traffic was over and the trip home took him only the eighteen minutes it usually did.

Or rather, as it *used* to do.

When he got home to Storsjövägen he backed up to the front entrance and shut off the engine. He climbed out and opened the boot. He had a lot to do today, and it was best he began at once.

*   *   *

The packing boxes lay in the cellar. He picked up four of them and took the lift up to the studio. It smelled stuffy when he opened the door, but he didn't feel like airing it. Instead he opened up two of the boxes and lined the bottoms with newspaper. The hibiscus had lost one of its two pink flowers, and the one that was left had withered into a shrivelled strip. He tossed the pot, dirt and all, into one of the cartons. For two years and five months he had seen to it that all her potted plants stayed alive, but now that was all over.

He was no longer responsible for their lives.

The boxes were heavier than he thought when they were full of dirt, and he had to drag them out to the lift. When he looked round one last time and made sure that all life in the flat had been emptied into boxes he closed the door behind him, locked both locks and threw the key through the mail slot.

Never again.

He continued to his own flat.

Some of the painting frames were too big to fit into the cartons, so he had to break them up.

When the walls were bare the flat looked completely naked. Just as naked and unblemished as he himself would be. He would cleanse every thought, every memory, clean every nook and cranny to make room for the love he had found.

Utterly pure and without guilt he would receive her, making himself worthy.

He opened the wardrobe and took out her clothes that he had brought down from the studio, shoving them down amongst the paintings. Her scent had long since left them, but they had still kept him company when the loneliness felt too oppressive.

Now he didn't need them any more.

Never again.

He had to put the last box on the passenger seat. The clock on the dashboard read only eleven thirty, and that was much too early. He would have to wait for evening in order not to attract too much attention. On the other hand, he would have to carry the boxes the last stretch of the way; it was only a matter of driving up to the Boat Club, and that would take him a while. He would rather have done it on the wharf, but he knew that was impossible. Yet he could do it on the beach right next to it. No one would see him from the path, but the bonfire would be visible from the south side facing Söder. But surely he could light a fire if he wanted to, and it would have to take place near the wharf.

Like a purification rite, once and for all.

On that September day two years and five months ago it had been raining for a whole week, but then like an omen the sky split open and turned bright blue two hours before she was to arrive. He had packed the picnic basket carefully. He had even made a quick trip down to Konsum and bought plastic champagne glasses so everything would be perfect.

As usual she was a bit late, twenty-six minutes to be exact, but she had wanted to finish something on a painting she was working on. It didn't make that much difference; if he had waited a year he could wait another twenty-six minutes.

He had placed a checked kitchen towel over the basket and during the walk down towards Årstaviken she kept asking him what was in it. As usual she babbled on; it bothered him a bit that she didn't seem to grasp the solemnity of the occasion. She talked about some gallery where she might get a chance to exhibit her paintings, and about how nice the man was who owned the place. The whole conversation made him uncomfortable. He hated it when she met people outside his control. He wanted to know everything she did, who she met and how she acted when she met them. A few weeks earlier he had mustered the courage to talk to her about it, explain how he felt. Something had happened after their talk, something that bothered him. For him everything he told her had been a sign of his boundless love, but somehow she must have misunderstood. It seemed as if she had pulled back the past few weeks. She had suddenly not been able to eat lunch with him as she usually did, and a few times she had pretended she wasn't home when he knocked on the door of the studio, even though he knew she was there.

Now he would see to it that everything was all right again.

He had thought that they should sit on the bench across from the Boat Club, but when she saw that the gates were open she absolutely had to walk out on the wharfs. She chose the one on the right, and they walked past the few boats that were still in the water, waiting to be taken out for the winter. They walked to the end, and he set the basket down on the concrete. The bench would have been better. She came over and stood by his side, looking out over the water.

A lock of her dark hair had slipped out of the clasp at the back of her neck and was lying across her cheek. He resisted the impulse to brush it aside, touch her face.

'God, it's so beautiful. Look at the Söder Hospital.'

He looked where she was pointing. The sun made the windows in the enormous white building glow as if fires had been lit inside each and every one of them.

'I should have brought along my sketch pad.'

He knelt down and took the towel off the basket, placed it like a tablecloth on the concrete, and set out the champagne glasses.

'Oh,' she said, smiling in surprise, 'it's a party!'

He felt the nervousness now, almost changed his mind. In some way she didn't seem fully there. Everything would be much easier if she met him halfway, tried to help him out. He took out the potato salad and the grilled chicken, reached for the sparkling wine and stood up.

Her smile. He had to touch her.

'What are we celebrating?'

He smiled at her, couldn't say the words, not yet.

'Has something wonderful happened?'

Now she was looking at him with curiosity, really looking at him. For the first time in weeks he had her full attention. Finally she was back again, with him, where she should always be.

He handed her the glass with determination.

'Will you marry me?'

He had fantasised about it for months. How her beautiful face would break into that smile that made her eyes narrow to slits. How she would come to him, come close, in complete trust and finally let him kiss her, touch her. She who had always had to struggle through life would understand that he intended to protect her, that he would never leave her, that she never had to be afraid again.

But all she did was shut her eyes.

She closed her eyes and shut him out.

A primal fear came over him. All the terror that she had protected him from for a whole year came flooding in like a great fury.

She opened her eyes and looked at him again.

'Jonas. We have to talk.'

She took the glass from him and put it down on the wharf.

'Come, let's sit down.'

He couldn't move.

'Come on.'

She reached out her hand and placed it carefully on his arm, led him cautiously over to the edge of the wharf and got him to sit down. She stared out over the water.

'I think the world of you, Jonas, I do, but what you said to me a few weeks ago scared me. I realised that maybe you've misinterpreted everything.'

I don't want you to live here any more.

'I've tried to explain things to you but . . . well, it's my own fault that it's gone this far, because I haven't dared, I didn't want to make you sad. Yes, and our friendship has been terribly important for me as well, I don't want to lose it.'

I don't want you to live here any more.

'This man at the gallery I told you about, his name is Martin, we have . . . he and I have . . . oh, damn it.'

She looked away but in the next instant he thought

he could feel her hand on his arm, though it could have been his imagination.

'I'm so sorry that I didn't say something sooner. I didn't realise how you felt until you told me that you didn't want me to see other people if you weren't with me. And this thing with Martin. Well, now I might as well tell you the truth. I really believe I can say that I love him. At any rate, I haven't ever felt like this before.'

He looked down at his arm. Yes, it was there. Her faithless hand lay there on his forearm.

She was touching him.

'Forgive me, Jonas, but . . .'

Everything went white.

In the next instant she was in the water. Her face broke the surface, shocked and furious.

'What the hell are you doing? Are you crazy?'

He looked around. There was an old abandoned oar next to him with only half the blade left. Her hands were clutching the edge of the wharf but he prised up her fingers so she had to let go. The next time he saw her head above the surface he shoved the oar against her shoulder and forced her back down. Her deceitful hands thrashed above the surface but vanished. Then she started moving out, backwards; she was trying to escape by swimming out of reach.

The water closed around him. The cold didn't touch him. Quickly he was at her side and shoved her head under the water. He fought off her thrashing arms and locked his legs around her to get extra leverage. It might have taken ten minutes; time did not exist. Only the feeling that she slowly but surely was ceasing to resist, had submitted to his will and given in.

And then the voice from somewhere that suddenly broke into his consciousness.

'Hello! Hello! Do you need help? I'm coming.'

She listened carefully while he was in the shower. When she heard him pull shut the shower door, she hurried into his office and copied the letters on the fax. Which of them would best suit her purpose she didn't know yet; she would take them with her and read them somewhere in peace and quiet when he thought she had gone to work.

She left only a note on the kitchen table – 'Going to work now, can pick up Axel today so you can work in peace and quiet.' – and with the originals back in the gun cabinet and the papers she needed stuffed into her briefcase, she pulled on her coat and left the house.

He was still in the shower.

Without consciously deciding which direction she would take, she drove out towards Värmdö, turned off on the road towards Gustavsberg and pulled into a parking space.

My love,

Every minute, every moment I am wherever you are. Merely the knowledge that you exist makes me happy. I live for the brief times we have together. I know that what we're doing is wrong, that we shouldn't feel the way we do, but how could I ever say no? I don't know how many times I've decided to try and forget you, but then you stand there in front of me and I just can't. If everything came out I would probably lose my job, you would lose your family, everything would be chaos. And yet I can't stop loving you. The instant I pray that all this had never happened, I'm scared to death that my prayer might be answered. I realise that I am ready to lose everything as long as I can be with you.

I love you, your L

The nausea grew stronger with every word she read. She had a parasite inside and she felt like puking, turning herself inside out to get rid of it. In an unguarded moment it had forced its way in and taken over her whole system, poisoned her family, and yet this was not punishable by law. There wasn't one line in the law books that could regulate the crime that had been committed. This woman had crushed a family and turned a child's parents against each other; the damage she had caused was unforgivable and could never be repaired.

She scanned one of the other letters but couldn't go on. The words she held in her hands consumed all the oxygen in the car, it was no longer possible to breathe. She tossed them onto the passenger seat and climbed out of the car to get some air.

She had a prickly sensation in her left arm.

Leaning forward with her eyes closed, she stood there with her hands flat on the bonnet. A car approached from the direction of Gustavsberg and she straightened up again. The last thing she wanted was for someone to stop and ask how she was. For anyone to see her at all.

When the car went past she saw the letters through the windscreen. They lay there in her car and she hated them, hated each and every black word printed on the white paper. Hated the fact that they were the same letters of the alphabet that she used, that she would always have to use.

Somewhere in the darkness she wondered about the passion that Henrik had managed to awaken in the other woman.

Why him, of all people?

What was it *she* saw?

Had she herself ever loved in the way that the words described? Maybe at first, but if so she couldn't remember. They had once, back when everything was different, decided to live their lives together, and to seal their decision they had brought a child into the world, a lifelong responsibility. And now, just because he was feeling a bit randy, it was all going to be shattered, all feeling of companionship abolished. As long as he could screw Axel's day-care teacher and get away with it, everything would be fine.

Fucking pig.

The anger came over her again and the prickling in her left arm subsided.

She was all decisiveness again.

She got into the car and picked up the first letter.

It was hard to believe that such a little poet was hidden behind that fey smile that greeted them every morning. On the other hand, the letter was perfect, didn't need the least bit of editing. And it was really eye-opening that she was ready to lose everything. That's what it said in black and white, and that was precisely what was going to happen.

Your prayer will be granted, little Linda, it most certainly will.

She looked at the clock. It was already a quarter past ten and time to drive back. By this time they would no doubt have set off on their picnic in the woods.

She started the car, made a U-turn, and drove back towards the day-care centre.

To be on the safe side, she left the car in the car park outside Ica and walked the last bit. No one could see her car in the vicinity of the day-care centre just now, no one would see her at all if it was avoidable. The playground at the back was deserted, the only things moving were the black tyres on their chains, swinging lightly in the breeze; otherwise everything was still. She wondered whether all the other children had gone too. That would definitely be best, as long as they hadn't locked all the doors behind them.

The street door to Axel's section was locked. She continued around the corner, passing the helter-skelter, and from a distance she could see that the door to the kitchen was held ajar with a blue plastic crate. Maybe Ines was busy preparing the afternoon snack. She walked the last bit to the door and listened at the opening. There was no sound other than a radio, and it seemed to be playing its music to an empty room.

If anyone happened to see her from one of the windows, she couldn't just stand there hesitating, she had to act as though it was completely normal for her to be at her son's day-care centre at five minutes past eleven on a Friday morning. Anyway, it wouldn't be a problem if someone asked. Finding a reasonable explanation for her presence was the least of her worries.

She opened the door and went inside. The kitchen was completely empty. Only three loaves of rye bread wrapped in plastic and a packet of Marlboro Lights on the stainless steel workbench in the middle of the room disturbed the order. The sound of a flushing toilet revealed where Ines was, and Eva hurried out into the corridor and down to Kerstin's office. No one in sight. She dashed past the staff room and the toddlers' section and in through the wide-open doors. Then she pulled them closed as quietly as she could and locked them. If anyone showed up, the locked doors would give her a few seconds' respite. She was actually just here to leave a message for Kerstin, and that was all anyone would see her doing if they unexpectedly interrupted her.

She went over to the desk.

She had never been a computer expert, but she should be able to work out how to start one of the computers. She put down her briefcase, pressed a button, and sat down in the chair to wait for the machine to boot up. Right in front of her was a notice-board with this autumn's group pictures from the four day-care sections. About sixty children and the staff that took care of them. Axel sitting cross-legged on the floor and just behind him the snake who had stolen his secure life. She stood up, leaned over the desk and regarded her enemy. Her blonde hair down over her shoulders. And that fucking smile. She wouldn't be smiling much longer.

She sat back down.

A window had appeared on the screen that asked

for her username and password. She keyed in Linda Persson and clicked down to password.

Usually three attempts were allowed; that's how it was with the server at work, at least.

Henrik. Please check your password. Axel. Wrong again. Bitch. Please contact community technical support.

She looked up at the notice-board again. Somewhere they must have the password written down so they wouldn't have to look it up in the internal catalogue, but maybe they knew it by heart. She picked up the phone and punched zero.

'School Board headquarters.'

'Hi, Kerstin Evertsson from Kortbacken pre-school. I've forgotten the number for computer technical support.'

'Four zero eleven. Shall I connect you?'

'No thanks.'

She hung up. She could ring internally herself to minimise the risk of arousing suspicion. She lifted the receiver and dialled the number.

'Computer support.'

'Yes, hi, this is Linda Persson from Kortbacken pre-school. We have a problem with our computer here and none of us can get into our email. It's something with the password.'

'I see, well, that's odd. What did you say your name was?'

'Linda Persson.'

The silence on the other end lasted a little too long.

'Can I call you back?'

The question made her hesitate. Would Ines in the kitchen hear the phone ring?

'Sure, but I'm in a bit of a hurry.'

'I'll ring in a couple of minutes.'

What choice did she have?

'OK.'

She put back the receiver but lifted it and pressed down the button with her finger instead. The shorter the ring the better.

The seconds dragged by.

Her sudden nervousness was consuming more energy than she could afford. How long would she be able to last without some sleep? Was it possible that she had been unlucky enough that the man she had talked to knew Linda, that he could hear it wasn't Linda on the line?

And then the phone rang.

'Kortbacken pre-school, Linda Persson.'

'Yes, this is computer support. Now, let's see. I've cleaned things up a little so there shouldn't be any problem. You just have to type a new password on the line and then confirm it three times in the dialogue boxes that come up afterwards. OK?'

'That's great. Thanks for your help.'

'No problem. That's what we're here for.'

Uh-huh.

She hung up the phone and tried to gather her wits again.

Linda's new password. That wasn't so hard.

She smiled to herself and typed the word in the dialogue box and then confirmed it three times according to the instructions.

And then she was in.

She quickly scrolled down through the inbox but couldn't find any mail from Henrik. Amongst the sent emails there was none to his address either. Either they only delivered their fucking letters by hand or else she used another email address when she was out seducing the kids' fathers. She was probably afraid of losing her job, that little bitch.

Ha!

She clicked on 'Write a new message,' opened her briefcase and took out the original letter and the address lists for the children in the day-care. It took her only a few minutes to type out the letter, even though she added a few typos, and then she started reading through the address list. Simon's pappa looked pretty good, he would get one. And then Jakob's pappa, that might make his wife less interested in organising the planning meetings before the damned Stone-Age camp.

She clicked on 'Send' and they were off.

There, Linda. It'll be very interesting to see how you explain this.

She turned off the computer, stuffed the letters back in her briefcase, and was just about to get up. Suddenly she heard the sound of footsteps approaching in the corridor outside, and she held her breath. The next moment the door handle was pushed down. She looked around. The room had no hiding places. The sound of keys rattling. With no time to think she slipped quickly out of the chair and crawled under the desk. The next instant the door opened, and she saw a pair of feet in indoor sandals approaching. As if the risk of being caught would be less if she closed her eyes, she shut them tight. At least she wouldn't have to see the expression on Ines's face if she found her under the desk. That mustn't happen!

The sound of paper being picked up on the desk above her head. Had she taken everything? What if she had forgotten something? Or what if Ines had to throw something in the wastebasket squeezed in next to her under the desk? Of course, there was absolutely no reasonable explanation for why she was under there. Why had she hidden? She was just leaving a message for Kerstin. If Ines saw her she would be lost. Her revenge would be revealed as soon as the email was read by the recipients. Good Lord, what had she done? A sudden sound made her open her eyes in pure terror. Ines's feet were only a few centimetres from her own. And then that sound again, longer this time. Her mind refused to decipher what she was hearing; maybe it was only a sound effect a second before the world found out about her miserable attempt. Then the feet in front of her hurried to the door and at the same instant her brain released the information: it was a doorbell she had heard. As soon as Ines left she crept out, her legs wobbly. She cast a glance at the desk to make sure she hadn't left any papers and then hurried toward the nearest exit, the one through Axel's section. The fatigue could no longer be held back, it felt like being inside a glass bubble; her world was shielded from what had once been called reality. The fear of being caught had used up the last of her adrenaline, which right now was the only thing keeping her on her feet. To keep going, she would have to force herself to risk sleeping for a while. Maybe in the car? Maybe if she drove off and parked somewhere safe, where nobody would find her?

She got into the car and started it.

A few hours' sleep.

She had to sleep.

First, sleep for a while and then she would drive home and put together a really nice Friday night dinner for her family.

He lay naked in the bed. The flat was cleaned and neat, he had only left the sheet untouched. The walls of the room were bare; everything that had hung there when he woke up this morning was gone. All that was left was a smouldering heap of ashes down by Årstaviken. And somewhere in Karolinska Hospital lay a body, but it no longer had anything to do with him. It meant as little to him as it had done three years and five months before, before he knew that it existed.

Soon it too would be ashes.

But his body was alive. For the first time it was alive and really alert. No longer like an enemy that he constantly had to deny, restrain, force back. All longing was suddenly permitted. The desire pulsing inside him was not a threat but a basis for all the fantastic things that awaited him.

He put his hand on his neck, then ran it slowly down over his chest and closed his eyes. Followed the memory of her hand and continued down over his belly. Just like this she had touched him. Just like this her hands had liberated him.

Why didn't she call?

The phone lay on the floor next to him at a right angle to the rug, and he no longer knew how many times he had looked at it, placed his hand on it as if it could reveal how much longer he would have to wait.

He wanted so much. He wanted so much and finally it was all possible, and yet it was almost more than he could bear to sit and wait. It was like torture.

He thought about all the wonderful possibilities that their meeting had created. Everything they could do together. Everything he had dreamed that he would do with Anna. It had all been taken away from him, and now he had been given a new chance. He would start working again, it shouldn't be difficult to get his job back as a postman, but that was only the beginning. Now he would realise his dream and take that course in trigonometry. He would sign up for it on Monday.

Why didn't she call?

He got up and went into the kitchen. The only thing edible in the refrigerator was a sausage wrapped in plastic with processed risotto. The date stamp said that it should have been eaten no later than the day before, but that couldn't be helped. He dumped the contents into a saucepan.

How could he have been so stupid not to ask for her phone number? What if she didn't dare ring? What if she thought he wasn't interested since he had fallen asleep without asking for her phone number? Damn it, he didn't even know her last name. What must she think?

It was so strange that they hadn't talked more. But actually he knew why. They had so much to say to each other that they chose to remain silent.

After all, they had all the time in the world.

What if she had been sitting there, hesitating with the receiver in her hand and didn't dare call? The thought made his stomach knot up. What an idiot he was for not asking! The only thing he knew about her was her first name. Her first name and the fact that he would never leave her. If he had to turn all of Stockholm upside down he would find her.

The thought of not knowing where she was was unbearable. If he didn't hear from her soon, it would come over him again, but for the time being he was safe. Her touch was still all over his skin, protecting him.

But for how long?

He had just put the first spoonful of risotto in his mouth when the phone rang. He rushed over to the sink, spat out the food and rinsed his mouth. He then dashed to the phone in the next room. Two rings.

Everything he had practised, everything he had planned to say, was all gone.

Four rings.

'Jonas.'

'Hi Jonas, this is Yvonne Palmgren at Karolinska. I just wanted to hear how things were going for you now.'

He sat in silence and felt the rage growing. There was nothing he wanted to say to this woman. She was ringing from another life that he had left behind. Nobody but Linda had the right to call him, no one had the right to block the line.

That bloody woman at the other end had asked him to let go and move on, and that was precisely what he had done. He had absolutely no obligations to report his feelings to her; he had done precisely what she asked him to do.

He hung up.

Shit. What if Linda had called just now and heard that the line was busy? She may have just gathered up the courage and finally dared ring him and then *it was busy*.

Fucking bitch!

He straightened the phone, which had been moved out of its right angle to the rug, pulled on a pair of slippers and went back to the kitchen. The risotto swelled up in his mouth, it was impossible to swallow.

What if he disappointed her, what if he couldn't live up to her expectations? What had she actually seen in him? What had made her, without suspicion, with such trust, come back to his flat with him and give herself to him, so utterly and without reservations? It must have been fate. They had found everything they were looking for when they met each other. That must be exactly how it feels to find the right person at last. All this couldn't have happened without a reason, it must have had a meaning. The fact that on that evening, the first one, he had met her and had dared let go. It was the beginning. He knew it!

Why didn't she call?

He got up and went to the phone to make sure he had replaced the receiver properly. He wanted to pick it up to make sure that the conversation with the Monster Psychotherapist had really been broken off, but he didn't dare. What if she tried to call right now?

He sat down on the edge of the bed.

What if he never saw her again? That thought was impossible to bear.

What if she didn't want to call, if that was why she

didn't wake him before she left? What if he had disappointed her? What if he had lost her?

It had to be worth something, had to be right. Otherwise Anna would win. Her betrayal would give her the revenge that he didn't deserve.

It had to be worth something! He had been so sure, felt so strong. Suddenly he no longer knew anything.

He couldn't stay in the flat, he had to go out. All these questions would drive him mad, he had to find her. Had to regain control of events.

He went to the wardrobe and took out a pair of beige trousers and a jumper. He ought to buy himself some new clothes, but how could he afford it? He wondered what kind of work she did. He had to find out. He had to find out everything about her. Be with her, share her thoughts, sleep with her. Everything. He wanted it all.

He took the underground to Slussen and walked the last stretch across to Gamla Stan. The clock on the Katarina Lift showed 21.32. He held his mobile in his hand so he'd definitely hear it if it rang; before he left the flat he had forwarded his home number. Halfway across Järntorget he stopped and looked at the red awnings. That was where she had been sitting. Yesterday he had stood right here on this square, and that was when it had all begun. Only twenty-four hours had passed since then, but everything was changed. Everything was new.

A man in his thirties, dressed in a suit, was sitting on the chair where he had sat, and on both sides of him were more well-dressed men. What if she were inside? What if he were only thirty metres away from her right this minute?

He started towards the door. The possibility that he might soon see her made him quicken his steps.

The bar was full of people. All the seats were taken, and there was a crowd along the bar area. He quickly swept his gaze across all the faces but she wasn't among them. That might be her over there, the one sitting with her back turned, in the black jumper. He forced his way forward through the crowd. In his haste he ran into someone's elbow sticking out, and the glass the person was holding sloshed over. An annoyed look. He didn't care. With heart pounding, he moved over to the opposite wall so he could see her face. And then the disappointment when he met the unfamiliar eyes.

It was unpleasant with so many people. A bustling hubbub in which no words could be heard, only waves of unfamiliar voices arching over the music.

Where was the toilet? Maybe she was in there. He continued past the bar and found two toilet doors in a hallway near the kitchen. The lock on one of them said Vacant, but to be on the safe side he opened the door to make sure she wasn't in there. The second said Occupied, and he took up position to wait, heard someone flushing. He saw her hand before him, felt how it caressed him over his hip and found its way further to his groin. The lust again.

He had to find her.

The lock was turned and showed green. He stopped breathing, closed his eyes for a moment. A woman in her fifties came out and he lowered his gaze. Where was she? Why didn't she come? One more time he checked the display on his phone. No missed messages. Maybe he shouldn't have left the flat. He was starting to regret it now, felt the compulsion enveloping him, pressing closer, ready to attack as soon as the slightest crack appeared in the shield she had given him. He looked at the door handle that he had just touched. Damn it. He touched it again to neutralise it, but that didn't help.

Luleå to Hudiksvall 612, Lund to Karlskrona 190. Fuck! Where was she?

He looked towards the bar. How many steps could it be? He had to have a beer or something to force these feelings back. There were no seats available and hardly any room either, but a little farther down stood a man in his late fifties who had drunk too much but was still trying to convince the barman to serve him another. He stood up in a rage when he was refused. The metal chair crashed to the floor and the noise effectively silenced all conversation. The music took over.

Everyone was staring.

The barman took the man's empty beer glass.

'You're done drinking for tonight. There won't be any more here.'

'You fucking little shit, give me another beer!'

'I'll have to ask you to leave now.'

The barman went over and put the glass in a rack for dirty dishes.

'For fuck's sake, what a shithole this is!'

The man looked around, searching for support in any of the eyes staring at him. Suddenly everyone was looking elsewhere, ignoring him. He didn't exist. Only Jonas kept looking, felt hatred towards the man standing there, looking so pathetic and letting himself be degraded. In a flash he saw another man at another bar.

People all started talking again as if on command. The noise level increased and the blur of words was back. The man hesitated a few seconds, holding on to the bar in an attempt to look halfway sober. And, finally, with as much dignity as he could muster, he reeled towards the door and vanished into the night.

The chair still lay on the floor, and Jonas went over and righted it. The recollection the man had triggered had for some strange reason made the compulsion abate. He was not like his father.

He sat down on the chair. The barman wiped the counter in front of him and gave him a quick look.

'Fucking riffraff.'

It was the same barman as the night before. The one who had served him and Linda. A tiny opportunity opened up.

'A beer. Not a light one.'

'A lager?'

'Whatever.'

'I'll get you a Harp.'

'OK.'

The barman reached for a glass from the rack above his head, filled it halfway and put it in front of him.

'Forty-two.'

Jonas took out his wallet and put a fifty-krona note on the bar. The barman went off to serve some other customers and Jonas took a few quick gulps before he emptied the rest of the bottle into his glass. The foam ran over the edge and made a little pool on the bar. He dipped his index finger in the liquid and wrote an L on the newly wiped surface.

He had to ask. It was his only chance. He would drink a little more, get a little buzz on so the compulsion wouldn't come at him if everything went to hell.

He was paying attention half an hour later. The barman was standing right in front of him, hanging up some clean glasses. Jonas was on to his third beer and was once again full of resolve.

'Say, I wonder if you could help me with something?'

'Sure.'

Glass after glass was moved from the tray to the overhead rack.

'It's like this: I met a girl here yesterday. I don't know if you remember that I was here last night.'

'Yeah, I remember. You were sitting over there.'

He nodded towards the short end of the bar.

Jonas nodded.

'Well, that girl . . .'

He broke off and looked down at the bar, then glanced up and smiled.

'Well, you know. We went home together and all that. And then I got her phone number and promised to call her, but I lost the piece of paper. This is embarrassing as hell.'

The barman smiled.

'Well, that's not so cool.'

'Do you remember her too?'

It was a really dumb question. Obviously he'd remember. No one who ever saw her would forget.

'You mean the one you bought a cider for?'

Jonas nodded.

'Linda is her name. Does she come here often?'

'Not as far as I know, at least I've never seen her before.'

Jonas felt his hope sink. This man and this place were his only link.

'So you don't know what her last name is?'

The barman shook his head.

'No idea. Sorry.'

Jonas swallowed.

The barman looked at him briefly and hung up his last glass, took the tray and left. Jonas pulled out his phone; the display was still blank. She knew his name and where he lived but she still hadn't called. He looked around – at all the unfamiliar mouths talking and laughing, all the eyes gazing at each other, all the hands. Where was she now? Was she sitting in some other bar, a place like this but somewhere else? The thought that she was with other people right now, that someone else's eyes at this moment were allowed to look on her, that her body might be on someone else's retina, inside someone else.

'Listen, maybe I can help you after all.'

He turned back to the bar. The barman stood in front of him with a receipt in his hand.

'She paid for her first glass with a credit card. Before you got here.'

His heart turned a somersault inside his chest. He reached out his hand and took the receipt.

'Take it easy. I need that back.'

He read the white slip of paper.

Handelsbanken.

She had added a tip of ten kronor and then she had signed it.

The barman was watching him.

'But didn't you say her name was Linda?'

He read the signature again. Refused to understand.

'This must be the wrong receipt.'

'No, I remember, it's hers. The pen ran out of ink halfway through, see.'

He nodded at the receipt. The last letters were written in different ink.

'This is definitely the woman you bought the cider for. But it might not be such a good idea to get in touch with her.'

The barman gave him a wry smile.

Jonas couldn't take his eyes off the utterly incomprehensible signature. The woman who had made him betray Anna, who helped her to carry out her unjust revenge, had lied to him. The name he had learned to love over the past twenty-four hours was a lie, a lie that pierced him to the core.

Her name was Eva.

Eva Wirenström-Berg.

Pork tenderloin au gratin and roasted garlic butter potatoes. And a nice Rioja from '89. A hundred and seventy-two kronor she had paid for it.

She might just as well have served the liquid from the toilet brush holder. The fact was, she had once thought about doing just that.

They didn't say a word to each other during the meal; all necessary communication was relayed through Axel. He was allowed to light the candles on the table and now he sat there in his special chair and thought they were having a cosy evening. He had no idea that the cosy evenings were over for good in this house, and that the man who had taken them away from him was sitting at his right side and gulping down his food, all so he could go back to his den as quickly as possible.

Henrik gave her a quick look, stood up and took his plate.

'Are you done?'

She nodded.

With his other hand he lifted up the oven-proof dish with the pork tenderloin and went over to the counter.

She just sat there, amazed that he hadn't burned himself; surely the dish was still hot.

With mute efficiency he began clearing the table, rinsing the dishes and putting them in the dishwasher.

The family dinner was over.

It had lasted seven minutes.

'Axel, your programme's starting. Come on, I'll turn on the TV.'

Axel slid down from his chair and they went into the living room.

She sat there with her wine glass; he had forgotten to take it from her when he cleared the table. The wine bottle was more than half full, he had hardly touched it.

The first time the phone rang it was a quarter to twelve. Axel had fallen asleep in front of the TV at about eight, and Eva carried him in to the double bed. The rest of the evening she had spent alone on the sofa, sitting there staring at the flickering pictures on the screen. When the phone rang, Henrik happened to be out of his fortress and in the bathroom. She reached the phone first.

'Eva,' she said.

Not a sound.

'Hello?'

Someone hung up.

She stood there with the receiver to her ear and felt the rage building. That fucking slut! She couldn't even leave them in peace on a Friday night when he was home with his family.

She heard him flush the toilet and the bathroom door opened. He stood in the doorway.

'Who was that?'

She put down the receiver and did her best to seem calm, leafing through a catalogue that lay on the kitchen counter.

'I don't know, they hung up.'

A shadow of uneasiness flitted across his face.

And then he vanished into his office again. The door was scarcely shut before the phone rang again, cutting through the silence.

She reached it first this time too.

'Yes?'

Again a click. And then another ring as soon as she put down the phone. This time she didn't say a word, she just stood there listening to someone breathing.

And then suddenly there was a voice.

'Hello?'

'Yes, this is Eva.'

'Hi, this is Annika Ekberg.'

Jakob's mother.

'Jakob's mother from day-care. Sorry for calling so late, you weren't in bed already, I hope.'

'No, no problem.'

'I just have to ask you something. This may sound crazy, but Åsa, Simon's mother, just called me and said that Lasse had received a strange email from Linda Persson at the day-care centre.'

'A strange email?'

'Yes, you could call it that. A love letter.'

'What?'

'That's right.'

'To Simon's father?'

'Yes, and that's not all. We checked our email and we got one too.'

'A love letter?'

'Exactly the same one they got, word for word. I assume it's for Kjelle and not me, but it wasn't clear. Kjelle is mad as hell. In the email it sounds like they have some kind of love affair going on.'

'Well, that doesn't make any sense.'

'No. I don't know what to do.'

'Don't you think it's some kind of mistake?'

'I don't know. It was sent from her email address at work. It's possible that she meant to send it to somebody else, but it seems rather stupid. And if it was some kind of joke, then it's not very funny.'

'No, it certainly isn't.'

'I just wanted to hear if Henrik got one too.'

She suddenly felt unusually alert.

'Wait just a second, I'll check. No, actually I'll have to hang up so we can go online. I'll ring you in a few minutes.'

'OK.'

She hung up. She wanted to do this in peace without having Jakob's mother on the line. A slight smile was spreading inside her in the dark when she went up to the door and opened it without knocking. The stone was rolling. Where she wanted it to stop she didn't know; for some reason she didn't even care. Everything was ruined anyway. The goal was to do harm in return. Punish him.

He was sitting at his desk with his hands in his lap and staring straight ahead. The computer had gone into standby, and some coloured circles were snaking across the screen. He turned his head a little when he heard her come in.

But he didn't look at her.

'Who was that?'

'Annika Ekberg. Jakob's mother from day-care. Have you checked your email recently?'

'What do you mean?'

'Well, this is completely incredible. Both Jakob's and Simon's fathers got love letters from Linda at day-care.'

Even his spine revealed his reaction. For a few seconds too long he sat perfectly still before he turned his head and looked at her. Just a quick glance; his eyes flicked timidly at hers and then back to the screen.

'Oh, really. What did it say?'

He had never been a very good liar. Couldn't he hear how he sounded? How his forced indifference was an insult to her intelligence.

'I don't know. They wanted you to check whether you got anything.'

She went over and stood by his side, well aware that this way he'd be forced to display the correspondents on his latest emails.

He recovered quickly.

'I just checked. There wasn't anything.'

'Check again.'

'Why?'

'See if you have something now.'

'I was just in to check it five minutes ago.'

He was irritated now. Irritated and scared.

This was quite enjoyable.

'Five minutes ago I was talking on the phone. You couldn't have checked it then, could you?'

He gave a deep sigh. Showed with all his body language how annoying he found her.

'OK, maybe it was eight minutes ago. I didn't look at the clock.'

'Why don't you want to check it?'

'Damn it, I told you I just checked!'

An unpleasant tone of voice. So scared and so easy to upset. Imagine how much better you'd feel if you made an effort and looked at the truth, you fucking coward.

'Give me the phone.'

'Who are you going to call?'

'Annika.'

He gave her the cordless phone and she glanced at the telephone list on the notice-board. Annika answered after the first ring.

'Hi, it's Eva.'

'How'd it go?'

'No, he didn't get anything, he says.'

There was silence on the line.

Henrik sat as if paralysed, staring at the writhing snake on the screen.

She was busy thinking of her next move. Then she smiled to herself, looked at the back of his head and began talking. Let each syllable stab into him like a knife.

'I still think we ought to give Linda a chance to explain herself. I have a hard time believing she meant to send those emails, but the rumour will probably spread like wildfire. I think we should phone everyone and arrange a meeting at the day-care on Sunday evening. I can take care of it if you want.'

She heard Jakob's mother sigh on the other end.

'I wouldn't want to be in her shoes at that meeting.'

If only you knew what she does with them off.

'No, me neither. Really. But what else can we do? This way at least she'll have a chance to explain.'

Henrik still sat as if paralysed when she hung up.

The back of his neck was flaming red from all those stabs.

She fell asleep right away that night. The exhaustion took its toll, but at the same time she felt secure again. In complete control. Nothing could touch her. Everything was already destroyed.

Plan A had gone to hell despite all her struggles in recent years. Now it was Plan B that mattered. She only needed to rethink it a bit. It was up to her if he succeeded in crushing her or not, her own choice. Not that she would ever give him the satisfaction. On the contrary, she would see to it that he paid for his betrayal, both financially and emotionally. She would crush *him* instead, and then when he was fully aware of what had happened it would be too late. Then he would be left standing there.

Alone.

She woke up when the phone rang. Automatically her eyes looked at the clock radio. Who the hell called people at 6.07 on Saturday morning? Didn't she have any manners?

She reached out for the cordless phone and answered before the second ring.

'Hello.'

Henrik turned over on his side with his back to her and slept on.

Someone was breathing in her ear.

'Hello?'

No answer.

She threw off the covers, got up and left the bedroom. In the office she closed the door behind her.

'Did you want something? If so, it's probably better to say what it is now that you've called and woken us up.'

Utter silence. Yet she could hear that she was still on the other end.

There was so much she had wanted to say. So many words screaming inside in the dark that wanted to get out. But she was forced to restrain herself, not reveal that she knew, otherwise she'd lose her advantage. Plan B would be ruined.

'You can go to hell!'

She hung up.

It was impossible to go back to sleep. She crept in under the covers again and lay for a while staring at the ceiling. Axel cuddled up to her, moving his warm body closer. She turned over on her side and looked at his beautiful, peaceful face. The sudden pressure over her ribcage caught her unaware. She took a few breaths to try and relieve the pain, but the air refused to stay in her lungs. It forced its way out as if unable to stand being inside.

She turned over on her back but the pain increased, radiating out into her left arm and forcing her to grimace. Don't cry, steel yourself now! Think of something, try to concentrate on something else.

Home. Metre by metre she moved through her childhood home, remembering every step on the stairs, the creak of each floorboard. The way the curved handle on the front door felt in her hand, the sound of Mamma's and Pappa's calm voices filtering up through the wooden floor in her room when she went to bed, the way the Bakelite light switch in the old servant's bedroom always slipped back if you didn't turn it round twice.

And then the annihilating knowledge that her own son would never be able to quell his anxiety as an adult by remembering his safe childhood home. She had put so much energy into trying to create a home for him.

He would scarcely remember that once they had been a complete family.

Her failure was unforgivable.

The punishment eternal.

But she had no intention of carrying the blame alone.

Eva.

Her name was Eva.

Why had she lied?

Why had she gone home with him, given him access to her body, made him completely and without reservation admit her into his life, allowed him to reveal himself to her?

He lay on his back in bed and stared up at the ceiling, lay in the bed where they had made love. Where he had made love to her and she had used him, consumed him like an object. Utterly without consideration she had forced her way into his world, knocked over everything, stolen all the desire he had managed to preserve so long and with such great effort.

She was one of them.

One of the women who ruined his family and took his mother away from him.

The strength he thought she had given him had in three letters been transformed into a place vulnerable to attack, an undefended hole leading straight into his deepest fear. The fear whose only equal opponent was the control. His own means of defence.

Like a physical attack he felt the compulsion boring into him. There was nothing left that could withstand it.

He had been so strong only a few hours ago.

Who was this woman, who had claimed the right to inflict this on him?

He had already looked up the phone number in the book.

She lived in Nacka.

A ten-minute drive.

But it was impossible for him to leave the flat.

The first time he dialled the number it was 11.44 at night. He was sitting naked on the bed and the phone stood at a right angle to the right corner of the rug. It rang twice. And then her voice gave sound to the lie.

'Eva.'

So she confessed.

He hung up and felt the rage rising. And then a quick push of the redial button.

'Yes.'

He hung up again. Why had she answered 'Yes' when he called? Her voice cut through him, awakened the devastating longing to live. The memory of her nakedness forced all the blood to his groin, where his desire grew. He lay back on the bed, unable to move. The urge was again an enemy that rose up to mock him and laugh at him.

You are not worthy. No one wants you.

Maybe he slept for a few hours, maybe not.

The next time he called, it was seven minutes past six.

He had to hear her voice.

'Hello.'

He had to.

'Hello?'

No one was going to take this away from him.

'Did you want something? If so, it's probably better to say what it is now that you've called and woken us up.'

He stopped breathing.

Woken *us* up.

Now that you've called and woken *us* up.

'You can go to hell!'

On the other end she hung up. She, who the night before had slept with her skin against his, she who had opened the world to a possibility, turned everything into anticipation.

Last night she had slept with someone else who was called *us*.

Who?

Who was the one who was worthy?

She stayed in bed all morning. When Axel woke up, Henrik followed him out to the living room and turned on the children's programme, but he hadn't come back to bed to steal another hour of sleep as he usually did. Instead she heard the door to the office close and the sound of the computer booting up.

The pain in her chest had subsided, only a vague ache was left.

When the digital numbers on the clock radio had progressed to a quarter to twelve, he suddenly stood in the doorway.

'I'm going out tonight. Micke wanted us to go out for a beer.'

She didn't answer. Just confirmed that his inability to lie was astounding, a pure insult.

'You do that.'

Then he was gone.

She got up, reached for her robe, and went into the kitchen. Axel was sitting on the floor rolling his rubber balls down an invisible course, and Henrik was sitting at the table reading the newspaper.

'I promised Annika I'd call round so we can have a meeting at the day-care tomorrow evening.'

He looked up at her.

'Why's that?'

'Well, what's the alternative?'

He ignored the question and went back to his paper. She continued.

'If I were Linda, I'd want a chance to explain myself. Wouldn't you?'

If I were Linda.

She silently scoffed.

That was just it.

He turned the page even though he hadn't read a word.

'I just don't understand what you have to do with all this. Why do you have to organise a meeting? You didn't get an email, did you?'

No. But there's a gun cabinet in my cellar full of disgusting love letters to you.

'Because it's Axel's day-care teacher we're talking about. You must realise that it will affect the situation at the day-care centre when this all comes out. If it's true that she sent all those emails, would you have any confidence in her?'

'It's her own business, isn't it?'

'Her own business? Sending unwanted love letters to the children's fathers?'

'Did my day-care teacher do that?' Axel was sitting still on the floor and weighing a light-green rubber ball in his hand.

Henrik gave her a look full of contempt. Or was it pure hatred she saw?

'Great. Just great.'

He got up and left the room. By now she had learned how many steps it took. Eleven from his place at the table to his office, twelve if he took time to close the door behind him.

This time it was twelve.

'What about my day-care teacher?'

She went over and sat down with Axel. Absentmindedly she took a red rubber ball from the floor and made it come out of his ear by magic.

'Wow! And I thought you only had green balls in your ears!'

He smiled.

'Do I have any in the other ear?'

She glanced quickly to the side to find another ball.

'No. The one in there hasn't finished growing yet. The green ones take a little longer to grow.'

She took the cordless phone and the day-care list out on to the balcony and sat there making her calls. She had pulled a cardigan over her shoulders. It was warm for March, and after she had sat there a while she took off the cardigan and put it on the bench. She looked at the pylons that stuck up a few hundred metres away like futuristic steel wonders from the nature preserve. Nicke and Nocke, Axel had dubbed them as soon as he learned to talk. Although they were a conspicuous contrast to the woods, she had always liked them; they were always a landmark for home. She remembered a business flight from Örebro. The meeting that was the reason for the trip had raised insoluble problems, and she had climbed aboard the plane full of stress and tension. It was past ten at night, and soon after they took off she could see the masts far off in the distance. And she remembered the feeling of being so far away but still able to see home, to Henrik and Axel and everything that was safe. It was a moment of clarity about what was really important in life.

But then the years had passed.

Sixteen times she explained that Linda had emailed unwanted love letters to some of the fathers in the day-care group, and that they needed to have a meeting on Sunday evening. After her seventh call the phone managed to ring before she dialled the next number.

'Hi Eva, it's Kerstin at day-care.'

She sounded sad. Sad and tired.

'I just spoke to Annika Ekberg and heard that you two talked yesterday.'

'Yes, she called me late last night.'

There was a brief pause and all she heard was a deep sigh.

'Linda is quite upset. She didn't send those emails. We don't know how it happened.'

'No, I must admit I was quite shocked. I have a hard time believing it's true. I mean that Linda would have an affair with any of the fathers at day-care. That's a bit much.'

She looked out over the garden and tried to find the words that were required to describe what she was feeling. A calm after having regained control. Like an invisible spider in a net that no one but she knew existed. At the same time she wondered what she needed the control for, where she was headed. A feeling of being totally present. The here and now was everything. The next breath, the next minute. Everything after that was impossible to imagine. A thick red line had been drawn with a marker in an imaginary datebook, and that line could never be erased. Never ever. The past and the future had been ripped apart and would never meet again. And she herself was in limbo in between.

A sound made her turn her head. Out of the corner of her eye she had caught sight of something moving. Something big that quickly vanished behind the shed at the corner of the garden. In her life before the line in the datebook, she would have heeded the warning and gone out to pour blood meal on the most strategic spots, but now it made no difference. As far as she was concerned, the deer could eat up every hint of growth, each carefully nourished plant. Nothing would ever bloom again in this garden.

'I heard that you suggested we should arrange a meeting tomorrow evening, and at first I was dubious but . . . There's probably no other solution. I just don't know how Linda is going to bear it. This will open up a lot of issues for her. She had a very hard time of it earlier, and that's why she moved to Stockholm. It's nothing we need to discuss in this case, but I did want you to know about it at least.'

Another deep sigh.

'I actually just called to ask you to stress, when you make your calls, that Linda is incredibly upset about all this, and that she did not send those emails.'

'Of course.'

Linda had a very hard time of it earlier, and that's why she moved to Stockholm.

Interesting. Extremely interesting. But whatever she had a hard time with, it apparently didn't teach her to respect the lives of other people. No, divide and conquer, go straight into the shower and put down your earrings. Take whatever you want, you can't be bothered if some family is destroyed.

No, little Linda. You can sit there with your sad story. Your hard time is only beginning.

On the other hand, it might be useful to find out what you were running away from when you moved to Stockholm.

Henrik had already left by four o'clock. Dressed up and clean-shaven and in a cloud of aftershave he went off to have a beer with Micke. He had spent most of the afternoon in his office, but at regular intervals he had come out and restlessly wandered about the house. Like an animal in a cage. And she was the hated zoo-keeper, the one he was dependent on but who saw to it that his captivity was maintained.

She put Axel to bed at eight and thankfully he went to sleep right away. The knowledge of who Henrik was with crept into her body, and nothing on TV could distract her from her fantasies. She wondered where they were, what they were doing, whether they were lying entwined together and whether he was cautiously consoling her. Giving her all the tenderness and love that once had been hers.

Henrik and Eva.

So long ago.

How had it come to this? When had it reached the point that everything was suddenly too late?

She was all alone. He had already found himself a new travelling companion to lean on, someone to whom he could calmly lay out the alternatives for the future. It was an intolerable feeling suddenly to be exchanged, rejected, replaced by someone who was apparently better at fulfilling his expectations from life. Which she had not been able to do. And not a word had he spoken about his disappointment. He didn't even intend to show her respect by explaining, giving her a fair chance to understand what had actually happened.

She turned off the TV and the room became black. She hadn't even thought to turn on a lamp, although darkness had already fallen.

She sat down in the easy chair in front of the picture window facing the balcony. It was black as coal outside. Not even the moon could manage to light up the garden she had declared dead. She turned on the reading lamp and reached for the book she had started reading before the line in the datebook. It lay unopened in her lap.

It didn't interest her any more.

Had Linda had a chance to read the email she had sent? She had written the text herself, after all. Eva wondered how they would react when they saw the familiar words, what Henrik would think when he recognised Linda's declaration of love that he kept behind lock and key in his gun cabinet. Maybe he would suspect something, but how could he ever dare ask? She smiled at the dilemma she had created for him. Well, Henrik, what are you going to do now? When your lawfully wedded, understanding wife and the mother of your son might possibly be your worst enemy.

She looked at her reflection in the black windowpane. Linda's words had taken up residence, uninvited, in her memory bank, burned their way in like a disfiguring tattoo. She knew that they would haunt her for the rest of her life.

I realise that I am ready to lose everything as long as I can be with you. I love you, your L.

To be allowed to be so loved.

To be allowed to be as loved as Henrik was.

She wondered how he had answered that letter. Whether he suddenly found words that he had never used before, never had any occasion to use. Words which during their entire marriage had been biding their time because they weren't needed. Words that were too big, too strong and powerful, exaggerated even, but that were finally given the opportunity to break free and be put to use.

To help him maintain and preserve what he had found.

To be allowed to be so loved.

And to dare to let oneself be loved that way.

She closed her eyes when she was forced to admit that what he was experiencing just now was what she had always dreamed of for herself. Real passion. The kind that could go straight through her and force her to let herself go completely, not be able to resist. The kind she had never ever experienced. To be able to love unconditionally and be loved in return without having to perform, be talented, be the best every second of her life. To be the one she really was behind the façade she had so successfully managed to construct, hiding her fear of failure. Of not being good enough. Of being abandoned.

You're so strong. How many times had she heard those words? She played her role so well that no one ever saw through her, no one ever got to see the other woman hiding in the background. She felt a longing to show all her weaknesses for once without losing everything. And not have to fight to deserve it, to dare to let someone all the way inside without being afraid.

If only someone would say 'I love you' to her and mean every syllable of it, and wish there were even greater words because not even 'I love you' was sufficient.

She took a breath and opened her eyes. The realisation had given her palpitations. She looked at her face in the black window-pane and was ashamed at her weakness. She was strong and independent and all the rest was nothing but romantic fancy.

And yet.

Was it possible that someone could love her that much?

Out of a sense of duty and guilt, she had not allowed herself to express her secret wish even to herself. Bound by her vows and commitments she had repressed her longing in a shameful corner and barred the door.

Out of loyalty to Henrik.

He was the one she had selected to share her life, the one with whom she had experienced so much. She would never be able to do him such wrong. She had tried to fill her time with work and conversations with friends that might give her everything she knew Henrik couldn't give her.

All to hold the family together.

Now she sat here, alone.

He had found everything she had dreamed of finding.

And he had lied to her as if their relationship had never existed, she and their life together had never existed, had never been worth a thing.

She sat there for a long time, staring into her own eyes until the face around them was distorted and transformed into the face of a stranger.

And then, suddenly, a movement outside. Something quite close out there passed like a shadow beyond her reflection. The terror came like an electric shock: there was someone standing on the balcony staring in at her. Quickly she turned off the lamp, got up and backed away. The pressure over her chest. It was pitch dark out there, only diffuse shadows from the branches of the trees against the dark sky. She stood with her back to the wall and didn't dare move. Someone had sneaked round the house, carefully climbed up onto the balcony, and stood there protected by the darkness, looking in at her, standing only a few metres from her and looking straight into her most secret thoughts.

A sudden longing for Henrik. For him to come home.

Cautiously she moved towards the kitchen with her eyes fixed on the black window. She backed away and hurried over to the phone on the kitchen counter and quickly pushed the speed-dial number for his mobile. Two rings, three, four. And then silence, as he turned it off.

Not even the voicemail went on.

She was alone.

Inside the house.

And out there on the balcony, in the pitch-black darkness, stood someone who knew it.

It was undeniably a lovely house she lived in, this woman who had lied to him. Probably a hundred years old with yellow wood panels and white gingerbread trim, surrounded by gnarled bare fruit trees waiting for spring. Two cars in the driveway, a Saab 9-5 combi and a white Golf. Both considerably newer models than his own old Mazda. Inside this well-to-do suburban idyll is where she lived, then, the woman who had misused his body and seduced his soul. She and the one who went under the designation 'us'.

He had parked the car a couple of blocks away and approached on foot. He had been in agony all morning before he left the flat, but when he finally ventured out on a foray it had gone surprisingly easily. Perhaps it was the new feeling inside him that helped him, the feeling that an injustice had been committed and that he was the victim; a need to defend himself against an external enemy instead of the inner one.

He passed the house's mailbox, a cobalt-blue metal contraption that required a key to be emptied, with a small opening that required two hands to stuff the mail inside. An object hated by all postmen and newspaper boys. And there they stood so beautifully, the names of the couple who shared the home he saw before him. Eva & Henrik Wirenström-Berg.

Eva and Henrik.

To the left of the house the lot extended into a wooded common, with only a low hedge in between. He looked around and, since there was not a soul in sight, he took his time as he stepped on to the common amongst the trees. He stood behind a tree trunk with his hands on the rough bark and looked in at the back side of the house. A balcony, a lawn, several fruit trees, flower beds, in the corner of the yard a yellow-painted shed. All well-tended and nicely laid out, someone's cherished home. With his eyes still fixed on the house he leaned his cheek against the tree, feeling its roughness against his skin, and a shiver went through him. He wondered whether she was behind the windowpanes. And if *he* was there, the one called Henrik who was worthy, even though she had been unfaithful.

A whore is what she was.

He may have stood for half an hour behind the tree trunk when the balcony door opened. At first he couldn't see who had opened it, but the next moment she stood before him. His reaction shocked him. He hated her, but suddenly having her right there before him aroused a desire unlike anything he had ever felt before. During all the years of longing, all the nights at the hospital with Anna's mute body close to his, he had never desired anything as much as the woman he saw before him. But he hated her; she had seduced him, used him. These irreconcilable feelings fought for space inside him, forcing him to take a tighter grip on the tree in order to stay upright at all.

So close now, and yet so far away.

Over there on the balcony she sat down; in one

hand she held a phone and in the other a white sheet of notebook paper. A light-blue cardigan hung over her shoulders.

At first she sat utterly still, looking out across the lawn. Then she straightened up, looked at the phone in her hand, and dialled a number. He couldn't hear what she was saying; only a few words reached him behind the tree trunk.

The conversation took perhaps five minutes, and as soon as she hung up she looked at the paper and dialled another number.

The realisation that he could watch her without her knowledge made him excited. She was exposed to his eyes and utterly defenceless; he had power over her. Again and again she dialled a new number, and he wondered who she was calling and what she was saying. He wanted to know. She looked serious as she talked, didn't smile once. Then she took off the light-blue cardigan and placed it beside her on the bench. He could see the contour of her breasts under her jumper, the breasts his hands had caressed only a couple of days ago. He wanted to have that cardigan that had just rested on her body, inhale the smell of it, put it on.

The phone in her hand rang. She pressed the button and he could hear her answer with her name. The name that she didn't want him to know. He had to hear what she was saying. Cautiously and with infinite slowness so that his movements wouldn't attract her attention, he moved forward through the trees. Then he reached the last tree trunk, the one bordering the yard. A couple of metres ahead of him was the yellow shed.

She looked down at the floor of the balcony.

He didn't hesitate but seized the moment and ran the short distance to the protective wall and slipped quickly behind it. Through the gap between the panels and the drainpipe he could see her with one eye, but her voice was still undetectable. He was too far away.

She made a few more calls before suddenly getting up and vanishing back through the balcony door. The light-blue cardigan still lay on the bench.

He stood there for a while, unsure what to do. The sun had disappeared behind the treetops of the common, and he was suddenly aware that he was cold. As long as she was in front of him, no physical sensations were able to reach him, but she'd gone. He wondered whether it had something to do with her aura. Something about her body shielded him.

He ran the short distance back into the trees, then he walked without hurrying out to the street to the front of the house and stopped. It was the other one he had come to have a look at. The one who evidently was named Henrik and who was included in the designation 'us'. So far he hadn't seen any sign of him. At a slow pace he again walked past the mailbox with their names on it. He realised that he couldn't stand there without attracting attention, so he started walking in the direction of the street where he had parked. He was feeling quite cold now, and when he got back to the car he turned up the heat all the way.

The thought of driving to his flat didn't appeal to him. It was as though a magnet were drawing him towards the yellow house with the white gingerbread trim. He put the car in gear and let the force- field draw him to it. He drove slowly a short distance around the neighbourhood and then he was back. She was inside. Along with her, the other, the one who was worthy.

Just as he passed the mailbox the front door opened. There he was.

His foot hit the brake without being told to do so by his brain. The man outside the front door locked it after him and looked curiously in his direction. Jonas turned his face away. He had wanted to see more, look more closely, but he didn't want to be seen. Not now. Not yet.

A hundred metres farther along was a roundabout. When Jonas passed the house on the way back, his superior was sitting in the Golf and just backing out of the driveway. Jonas slowed down and let him back out. A hand in the side window waved to thank him; Jonas nodded slightly in acknowledgement.

You're welcome. I've fucked your woman too.

He followed at a safe distance. From the irregular streets of the residential neighbourhood to the motorway leading towards the city. He kept a few cars in between them. No one must know that he was there, watching, checking, in control. Calm filled him. The compulsion was far away.

After Danvikstull they turned off to the left towards the newly built-up area in Norra Hammarbyhamn, first to the right and then right again. He knew this part of Södermalm. He had filled in there for a week several years ago when half the city called in sick during a flu epidemic. The car in front of him turned right up Duvnäsgatan and vanished out of sight for a moment. Jonas slowed down when he saw it pull into a parking space but kept going straight ahead, parked and climbed out. He rounded the corner towards Duvnäsgatan and at the same moment the other man's car door opened. A blonde woman about his age, maybe a couple of years older, came out of the building about ten metres farther down. Jonas pulled up his hood and started walking up the hill on the other side of the street, stopped by a shop window across from the parked Golf and stood there. He could see them in the reflection in the window, and nothing would ever surprise him again. The pieces didn't fit together any more. For a brief second his eyes re-focused and he suddenly read a sign inside the shop window: 'To Let'. There was nothing else displayed in the empty window. But the reflection had even more to reveal. The woman who had just come out of the building and the man named Henrik who had just left his beautiful suburban home now stood embracing each other across the street. Quite still and almost convulsively they held on to each other, as if they might fall over if either of them let go.

They stood there like that for a long time. Long enough for him to attract attention in front of the empty shop window if they were capable of noticing anything outside their own sphere.

Who was this man? In the house he had just left, a woman was walking around who was everything a man could desire. And yet he stood here across the street in another's embrace.

Without turning round Jonas started walking down the hill, back to his car. He felt confused now, wondering about what he had seen, and whether everything was as it seemed. A husband and wife who satisfied their desires elsewhere, with other partners.

Bloody hell.

He'd never put up with that.

The day he got married and someone really loved him for the person he was, the day someone truly saw him, he would never again look at anyone else. He would drag out all the passion inside him and make his woman a queen. He would worship her, do everything she asked, be there loving her every second. He would never fail. His love could work miracles if someone would only let it. If anyone would only accept it. Why could no woman see his capacity, see the inherent power in him? Why was there no one who wanted to accept all that he had to give?

Anna had known. And yet he wasn't good enough for her.

A great longing came over him again, a longing for a way out of his loneliness. And then he thought of the man named Henrik, whom he had just seen in the other woman's arms. A man who had everything anyone could ever want but was still not satisfied.

And Lind . . . Eva.

Eva.

What was it she had wanted of him when she went home with him?

Out of the corner of his eye he saw a car pass by his side window, but not until it was gone did he realise it was the Golf. The woman was sitting in the passenger seat.

He turned the key in the ignition and almost automatically rather than by making a conscious decision, he followed. Renstiernas Gata on the left and then Ringvägen to the turn-off at Nynäsvägen. He didn't care about keeping his distance any more, he might as well drive where he liked.

In fact he ended up driving all the way to a little out-of-the-way pizzeria halfway to Nynäshamn. A hundred metres ahead he saw the Golf turn in and park. The restaurant didn't look particularly luxurious or cosy, so he assumed it had been chosen because of its safe distance from the house in Nacka. Infidelity apparently required a certain caution. He knew that better than most. He felt his disgust grow when he saw them walk inside. His arm around her shoulders, protective, attentive. How could a woman be so stupid as to trust a man who at that very moment was betraying another woman?

It was all so incomprehensible.

He waited a while before he left his car, in no hurry as he read the laminated menu beside the door. They were seated facing each other at a table in the corner, and a man with a foreign appearance was taking their order. There didn't seem to be much of a rush at the place, because only two other tables were occupied. At one table sat three teenage boys barely old enough to be drinking the beer they held. At the other sat a family with children who had just finished eating. And yet it wouldn't seem too odd if he picked the table right next to them. He took a few steps to the table and just as he pulled out the chair he saw out of the corner of his eye the man named Henrik who was being unfaithful give back the menu. Jonas sat down and a second later he had the same menu in his hands.

His hands.

The hands that had caressed the same woman.

His own in unconditional love, the other man's in unconditional betrayal.

And yet it was he, the other man, who had the right to touch her.

He pushed aside the menu on the table, not wanting to touch it. He tried to remember the name of some type of pizza from the text he had read on the placard outside the front door.

Then the man with the foreign appearance went back to the kitchen and the others started talking to each other. Without straining he could hear every word of their conversation even though they lowered their voices. And suddenly it was all so clear. Why everything had happened. Why it was predestined that he should catch sight of her when she was sitting under the red awning the evening before last, why the two of them should meet.

He had been given a task to perform.

He who believed that she had been sent to save him. It was precisely the opposite! He was sent to save her. Their deceitful, merciless judgement over two mediocre Quattro Stagioni pizzas. She, who wasn't even here to speak for herself.

He couldn't eat the pizza he had ordered. He left it untouched and asked for the check.

Their voices echoed in his head during the trip back towards Nacka.

'When do you intend to tell her about us? I just can't stand to go on like this much longer.'

'I know. But there's also Axel to consider. I have to arrange for a flat first so he can live with me as well.'

And that was when he had understood that somewhere in the midst of all this self-absorption there was a son.

There was a son.

And here at a suburban pizzeria, hidden away in fear that someone might see him, sat his father with a whore eating pizza.

It was dark by the time he turned onto the street where he knew she lived. He stood outside the car and watched in fascination the play of lights from the top of the Nacka Masts a few hundred metres off. The sweeping lights that branched like straight streets through the cloud cover to vanish softly into infinity. Of course she lived underneath a searchlight, but all she had to do was head towards the light.

This time he walked straight onto the property, stopping at each window to peer cautiously through the darkened panes on his way round the house. He didn't see her anywhere. Then he reached the back yard and saw the glow of a lamp through the big window next to the balcony door. He walked out onto the lawn so he wouldn't come too close, not wanting to risk her catching sight of him. Not yet. Not until he was ready.

Then he finally saw her. With only a reading lamp lit she was sitting in an easy chair right next to the window. For a second or two he thought she was staring straight at him, but then he realised that her eyes were staring into the darkness surrounding him. He couldn't resist moving closer. Step by step, with infinite slowness, he approached the balcony. Three steps up the stairs and then he was close to her. Right up close. Only a window-pane prevented him from reaching out and touching her. A book lay unopened on her lap, and he looked at her hands lying folded on top of it. The same hands that had caressed him and made him come alive. He had only one wish: to feel those hands against his skin once more. He had to subdue his desire, give her a chance to try and understand. He raised his gaze to her face. It was utterly devoid of expression, but then he saw that tears were running down her cheeks like white tracks against her skin.

O beloved, if I could only hold you in my arms. Don't be afraid, I'm here with you, I'll watch over you. I will prove my love to you. And when you understand what I'm prepared to do to win your love, then you will love me in return. Forever. And I shall never leave you. Never.

He suddenly felt his own eyes brimming over with gratitude. The two of them, together in tears, only a few metres apart.

Not even the thought of a night alone in the flat could frighten him now.

Secure in this knowledge he backed away, rounded the corner of the house and returned to his car.

Who knew better than he what betrayal could do to a woman? Or what was required in order to save her.

This time he would not fail.

He had been given one more chance.

She hadn't slept a wink when she finally heard his key in the front door. In the dark she had restlessly paced back and forth past the windows facing the garden. She had sensed not a movement, not a sound, only pale shadows from the trees when the moon peeked out occasionally from the banks of clouds. And then the veiled, sweeping glow of the lights from the Nacka Masts.

As soon as she heard him coming she hurried into the bedroom and got in bed next to Axel. It was past four o'clock.

He was taking his time in the bathroom. Almost half an hour passed before she heard him come up the stairs and a minute later he lay down on the other side of the double bed. Only then did she turn over and pretend to be waking up.

'Hi.'

'Hi.'

He turned over on his side with his back to her.

'Did you have a good time?'

'Mmm.'

'How was it with Micke?'

'It was OK. Good night.'

By Sunday morning she noticed that there was something he wanted to say. His restless pacing from room to room continued, but he spent more and more time outside his office and actually in the same room as her. She didn't intend to help him start the dialogue; she enjoyed watching him struggle. Finally, at the kitchen table over a quickly prepared lunch-time omelette, he summoned his courage. Axel, in his special chair at the end of the table, would serve as a shield in case of any conflict.

'I thought about what you said, that maybe I should go away for a few days.'

She chose to sit in silence, taking Axel's knife and helping him to scrape up the last remnants on his plate into an easily attacked pile.

'I'm leaving on Monday morning if that's OK. Just a couple of days.'

'Of course. Where are you going?'

'I'm not quite sure. I'll just take the car and drive.'

'Alone, or . . .'

'Yes.'

Lying 101: To lie successfully, don't answer a question too quickly. What an idiot.

She got up and began collecting the dishes.

'You know there's a meeting at day-care this evening, don't you? I thought I'd ask Axel to stay with Mamma and Pappa so the two of us can go together.'

She saw him swallow.

'I talked to Kerstin. Linda is apparently quite beside herself, poor thing. She has assured everybody that she wasn't the one who sent those emails.'

He picked up his water glass and took a sip as she continued.

'Do you know how that stuff works? Can someone else really go in and use her email programme?'

He got up and went over to put his glass in the dishwasher.

'Evidently.'

Now he had obviously said all he was going to say. She realised that if she wanted him to say anything else she would have to do it now. Before he managed to take those twelve steps to his office.

'But why would anyone want to do such a thing to her? The whole thing is just unbelievable, I mean she could lose her job over something like that. If someone's playing a joke, then I have to say she must have odd friends.'

He didn't intend to discuss the matter any longer, that was clear. The first seven steps across the floor towards sanctuary were already taken.

Her parents offered to come and fetch Axel, and the thought that Henrik might be forced to have a cup of coffee with his in-laws appealed to her. She baked a sponge cake and set the table in the living room to make it extra festive.

It took a while before Henrik joined them. He stayed behind his closed door as long as he could, and when he finally came and sat down his coffee was already cold. He went to the kitchen to empty his cup and then came back and sat down.

'I suppose congratulations are in order.'

Her father had Axel on his lap.

'Eva tells me you're writing a big article for some magazine.'

Henrik gave his father-in-law a blank look.

'Well, we heard that you celebrated the other day,' her father continued in explanation.

Henrik glanced at Eva. She didn't intend to help him out.

'Oh yes, that one. Of course.'

'Which magazine is it for?'

'Oh, it's a new one. I'm not sure of the name.'

And with that the topic was exhausted. Henrik drank his fresh coffee in silence, and her parents did their best to keep the conversation going. Eva mostly sat in amazement at the situation. This might be the last time they all sat here together. The last time.

Soon she would have to tell them, talk to them about money. She would need their help when she threw him out of the house.

But it wasn't quite time for that yet.

'Well, I suppose we should be heading home.'

It was not a question but a statement. She realised that they had all been sitting in utter silence at the table for quite a while, and when she glanced up her mother was looking at her. Her father's chair scraped against the floor when he got up.

'What do you say, Axel, would you like to come home with us while Mamma and Pappa go to a meeting?'

Eva began gathering up the coffee cups.

'Axel, if you want to take something with you for Grandma and Grandpa, please go and get it. You can take the rucksack if you like.'

She picked up the plate with the sponge cake, which only Axel had sampled, and went out to the kitchen.

She heard Henrik take the opportunity to flee once more.

'I'd better go back in and do some work. Bye, Axel, we'll see you this evening.'

He passed by her outside the kitchen doorway without giving her so much as a glance.

It was a couple of hours until the meeting started. She sat down at the kitchen table with one of the stacks of papers from the kitchen counter. Unsorted mail, mostly in window envelopes, most of them to Henrik. It was a long time since he had opened any of them himself. Afraid that they would sit too long and that a bill might be paid late, she had started doing it for him. Neither of them had ever mentioned it. As with so much else. She would never dare relinquish control when it came to the bills, firmly convinced that he wouldn't pay a single one on time. How could he if he didn't even manage to open his own mail? And yet there was an unspoken desire that he should take greater responsibility for paying them.

Should have taken greater responsibility, that is.

That problem, like so many others, would soon be moot.

She looked around. She had expended so much effort, so much energy. The old drop-leaf table: how many antique shops had she visited before she found exactly the one she wanted? The pot on the floor that she managed to drag home from a holiday in Morocco. It had seemed so insanely important that she even paid an excess baggage fee because her suitcase was too heavy. The painting from her childhood home, the chairs that had cost a fortune, the canisters on the kitchen shelf that she never used but that stood there to add a homely touch. Everything suddenly felt spoiled. As if the familiar objects had been transformed and she was seeing them for the first time.

Not one item moved her any longer. She couldn't even remember how it had felt when they were important. All she had taken for granted was herself. Everything she had thought and valued, everything that had moved her, none of it was right any longer. It was as if a lens had been slid into place for her alone, making everything look different. Only she could see how meaningless it actually was. She was completely alone, her own world right next to the one that belonged to everyone else. And yet she sat there as usual and paid bills to the world outside.

The door to the office opened. He went into the living room but came right back, picked up a toy from the floor and put it on the kitchen counter and disappeared into his office again.

She glanced through a brochure from the Council, put it in the pile to recycle, and opened the next envelope.

Then he came out again and made another round for no apparent reason. When he did it the third time a few minutes later she couldn't restrain herself any longer.

'Are you restless?'

She tore out the window from the envelope and put what was left in the recycling pile.

He probably imagined she said 'Hurry back into your office and don't come out again until it's time to leave,' because that was exactly what he did.

Evidently it was too much to expect an answer to her question.

Then it was finally time. She felt in unusually high

spirits, as if they were on their way to some long-anticipated celebration.

He drove and she sat next to him in the Golf; it was more practical. For that matter, he could take it with him; the Saab was hers and had been paid for by the firm.

'By the way, I'm sorry I made you lie to Pappa. About the job. That's not what I intended.'

He didn't answer. His eyes were fixed straight ahead, his hands on the wheel at ten to two.

She continued.

'I just didn't feel like telling him what was going on last Thursday when Axel slept over. That we needed to have some time alone, you and I.'

Some sort of sound came out of him this time, no words but more like a grunt.

She smiled slightly into the darkness and put her hand familiarly over his on the gearstick.

You're so good at lying. I had no idea.'

The playroom was already filled with parents with light-blue plastic booties pulled over their shoes. Chairs had been set out on the green floor, but most of the parents were standing in groups and talking in low voices. Neither Kerstin or Linda could be seen. Henrik went over and took a chair by the door. His fingers were drumming nervously against the side of the chair.

Eva went over to Jakob's mother and looked around.

'It seems as if most people thought it was a good idea to have a meeting.'

Annika Ekberg nodded.

'Yes, they did. Thanks for your help.'

'Don't mention it.'

The murmuring stopped when Kerstin appeared in the doorway. No one in the room could claim that she looked very happy.

'Hi everyone, and I'll say welcome even though it's not exactly a pleasant occasion this evening. Well, you might as well take your seats.'

Like obedient day-care children they did as she asked. Thirty-two parents in their plastic-bootied feet sat down. Eva's chair stood next to that of her lawfully wedded husband.

'As I'm sure you all understand, Linda is finding all this incredibly trying. Once again I'd like to assure you that she wasn't the one who sent you those emails; none of us has any idea how it happened. The Council's computer department will be starting its investigation first thing tomorrow morning. It wasn't possible to get hold of anyone over the weekend.'

'Isn't Linda here?'

It was Simon's mother who asked. Her tone was full of mistrust, and it was obvious to everyone in the room that she definitely did not appreciate the love letter to her husband.

Welcome to the club.

'Yes, here she comes now. I just want to say one thing first.'

She stepped aside and made room for Linda, who appeared in the doorway, head bowed. Kerstin placed an arm protectively round her shoulders, and the contact made Linda sniffle a bit. Eva saw Henrik clenching his hands out of the corner of her eye.

Linda cleared her throat but kept her gaze fixed on the padded rug.

Go ahead and look. It won't help you.

Then she opened her mouth to speak in her defence.

'I don't know what to say.'

The room was dead silent. For a long time it was quiet, long enough to make her start crying in earnest. She hid her face in one hand and Henrik squirmed uncomfortably in his chair.

'Is there anyone beside you who has access to your email?'

Eva didn't recognise the voice asking the question behind her back.

'No, not that I know of, and now I can't get into it myself any longer. It seems as if the password has been changed.'

Try cock-teaser.

There was another silence, but not as long this time.

'So what was in the emails?'

A female voice this time, also unfamiliar.

'I don't know. As I said, I didn't write them and didn't read them either.'

'I can read it out loud if you like.'

Simon's father took a folded piece of paper from his jacket pocket and cleared his throat before he began to read, dry and matter-of-fact, as if from the minutes of a board meeting.

My love,

Every minute, every moment I am wherever you are. Merely the knowledge that you exist makes me happy. I live for the brief times we have together. I know that what we're doing is wrong, that we shouldn't feel the way we do, but how could I ever say no? I don't know how many times I've decided to try and forget you, but then you stand there in front of me and I just can't. If everything came out I would probably lose my job, you would lose your family, everything would be chaos. And yet I can't stop loving you. The instant I pray that all this had never happened, I'm scared to death that my prayer might be answered. I realise that I am ready to lose everything as long as I can be with you.

I love you, your L

It was as if the very air in the room were transformed as he read it aloud. With each syllable he read, Linda raised her eyes centimetre by centimetre until she met Henrik's. Eva turned a bit so she could look at him. His expression was impossible to read. Terror-stricken was the first word that popped into her mind. Then he turned to her and for the first time in a long while they looked at each other. And she saw that he was afraid. Afraid that his suspicions might turn out to be true. That she knew everything. Then she smiled to him and stood up.

'Listen, everyone, I'd like to say one thing if it's OK. Since it's obvious that Linda didn't send these emails, we have to believe what she says. I mean, just imagine if you were subjected to something like this and then had to stand up in front of all of us and defend yourself.'

She turned to Linda.

'I truly understand that this must be hell for you. I think you have shown tremendous courage to meet with us all today.'

But shut your trap, you goddamn bitch, before you start slobbering too.

She turned to the group again.

'What do you say? We might as well let that computer department figure this out, then we can try and forget it ever happened. We have to think of the children above all else. Don't you agree?'

A faint murmur and then some who began nodding. Henrik had assumed the same expression as Linda and sat with his mouth open, staring at her.

Yet another common feature they could build their future upon.

Simon's mother was the only one who seemed to have another opinion. That this shouldn't just be forgotten as if it had never happened.

Eva turned to Linda and Kerstin, and smiled. Kerstin gratefully acknowledged her smile, and perhaps that's what Linda was trying to do as well, it was hard to tell.

Kerstin took a step forward and put her hand on Eva's arm.

'Thank you, Eva, thank you very much.'

She let her gaze wander over the crowd of parents.

'Linda has asked for a few days off next week, and I think that's a good idea. She might need a little rest after all this.'

Eva glanced at Henrik, who was now sitting and staring at the floor. She knew that he would never dare ask her whether his suspicions were true. That would mean admitting what a cowardly and lying jerk he was.

She was still in control.

And the next morning she would wave good-bye

to him from their driveway and say how much she hoped he would have a good time on holiday, and above all she would ask him to drive carefully.

She would have a full schedule while he was gone.

He was standing amongst the trees on the common when the Golf drove up the driveway. An unsettling revulsion had come over him when he realised that the house was empty, that he didn't know where she was. As soon as the car came to a stop the door on the driver's side opened and the man named Henrik climbed out and walked quickly towards the house. She remained sitting in the passenger seat, and when the car door was opened and the overhead light went on, he could swear that she was smiling. Then she got out, stood for a moment by the car and appeared to be in no hurry to reach the front door. The instant she put her hand on the door handle, he punched in the speed-dial number on his phone, and just as she disappeared into the house he heard the voice in his ear.

'Henrik.'

'Is this Henrik Wirenström-Berg?'

'Yes.'

He picked off a piece of bark on the tree in front of him. He was in no hurry.

'Are you alone?'

'What?'

'I mean, can you talk undisturbed?'

'With whom am I speaking?'

'Pardon me, my name is Anders and . . .'

He made a little pause for effect before he continued.

'I have something I'd like to speak with you about.'

'Oh yes? And what would that be?'

'It would be best if we could meet somewhere. I'd rather not talk about it on the phone.'

There was silence on the line. He heard porcelain rattling in the background and then the sound of a door closing. A lamp was turned on in one of the windows on the side of the house he was facing.

'And what does this regard?'

'I can meet you tomorrow whenever and wherever you like. Just tell me a time and place and I'll see you there.'

'Tomorrow I'm busy.'

I know that, you stupid idiot. But you can make it before the ferry leaves.

'How about on Tuesday?'

'I can't do it then either. I'll be out of town for a few days.'

He didn't intend to wait that long, he wouldn't be able to stand it. Somehow he had to arrange a meeting, but how much should he say? It went against the grain for him to plead with the pig on the other end, but the thought that he was doing it for her sake made him conquer his distaste.

'Henrik, it's best for both of us if we meet as soon as possible, you and I.'

And then when he didn't get a response, a little hint to put on the pressure:

'I just can't stand going behind your back any longer.'

The silence that followed confirmed that his words

had hit home. It had been an innocuous statement. How could a man who was unfaithful know what might be going on behind his back? But the fact that someone was doing something behind his back, since he was doing the very same thing, might interest him enough to agree to a meeting.

Then he cleared his throat.

'I can meet you at nine tomorrow morning. In front of the main entrance to the Viking Line terminal at Stadsgården. What do you look like?'

'No problem, I'll recognise you. I'll see you at nine.'

He hung up, looking towards the lighted window with a smile, and went back to his car.

He had seldom had such a calm night, and for the first time in ages he awoke thoroughly rested. He spent a long time picking out his clothes. It was important that he be dressed properly; Henrik had to understand that he had been outmanoeuvred by a man who was superior to him. He didn't want to take off the light-blue cardigan he had slept in; he was well aware of what had prompted his calm. It still smelled faintly of her, but he knew that it was a transitory security.

The phone rang.

He looked at his watch. It was only seven a.m. Who would call so early on a Monday morning? Not until he picked up the receiver did he realise that he hadn't even counted the rings.

'Jonas.'

'Hi, Jonas. This is Yvonne Palmgren at Karolinska.'

He couldn't say a word, only gasp furiously for breath. This time she apparently didn't intend to let him cut her off.

'I want to meet with you, Jonas. Anna's funeral is on Saturday and it's important that you be included in the process.'

'What process? Do you want me to dig the grave or what?'

He heard her take a breath.

'We're going to hold the funeral ceremony here at the hospital chapel, and I would like you to be involved in the planning. How she should be dressed, what kind of music to play, what kind of flowers to have, how to decorate the casket; no one knows better what she liked.'

'Ask Dr Sahlstedt. According to him, she couldn't even feel anything before she died, so I have a hard time believing that she would suddenly start caring now. By the way, I'm booked up this week.'

He hung up and had to admit, annoyed, that the conversation had got to him. Bothered him. The only way to deal with it was to counter-attack. He went out in the hall, picked up his wallet and took out the yellow Post-It note that Sahlstedt had given him. She answered after the first ring.

'Jonas here. I just want to say that if you or anyone else ever calls me again about Anna or anything to do with her then I'll . . . I have absolutely no obligations with regard to her, and for God's sake, I've done more than anyone could ask for that fucking whore. Do you understand what I'm saying?'

There was a pause before she replied. When she finally began to speak she did so calmly but with emphasis, as if every word were underscored with a red pen. A contemptuous tone, as if he were inferior to her.

'You're making a big mistake, Jonas.'

The loathing he felt overflowed.

'One more word and swear I'll make sure you . . .'

He broke off and regretted the words the instant he said them. He shouldn't be rash, shouldn't reveal to people who had no business knowing, that he was the one who had the power now. Then it might be used against him.

He hung up, stood still for a moment to catch his breath. He didn't manage to collect himself enough to go back to the wardrobe until he had pulled on the light-blue cardigan again and laid down on the bed for a while. It took him a very long time to obliterate the thoughts of that unwelcome conversation.

He got to the meeting place in good time, a half hour earlier than they had agreed. He wanted to have a complete overview, be prepared, see Henrik coming and be the one to choose how and when he would make the first move to contact him. He wondered whether Henrik would come alone or bring the whore with him; it probably didn't make any difference, but he would prefer to meet him alone. Their boat wouldn't be going until a quarter past ten. With his own ears he had heard them mention the departure time during the conversation in the pizzeria.

It was a simple matter to vanish in the crowd of people in the bowels of the terminal. He sat down on a bench next to a bunch of middle-aged, hungover Finns in jogging suits, where he could see the main entrance. And then at five to nine Henrik appeared, alone. Just inside the doors he stopped, put down a well-packed bag on the floor, and looked around.

Jonas bided his time, wanting to let him wait for a while. Watched him look at his watch over and over, turning and twisting in all directions and closely studying all the men passing by.

Jonas closed his eyes and took a deep breath in the dark, resting a moment in the calm that filled him. Knowing for the first time what awaited him. That the future would be his reward for all his struggles up to this day. That the fear could not reach him any more. The feeling was as unfamiliar as it was welcome, so utterly liberating, an all-encompassing grace.

Then he got up and started walking towards his enemy.

He stopped a metre from him but said nothing, let him keep wondering. At last it was the other man who broke the silence.

'Are you Anders?'

He nodded but chose to remain silent. The enjoyment of the other man's obvious discomfort was too much to resist.

'What was it you wanted? I'm in a bit of a rush.'

This time he sounded annoyed.

'Thank you for taking the time to meet.'

Jonas didn't intend to let himself be hurried. Instead he smiled a little. Maybe his expression would be interpreted as arrogant, but that wasn't really his intention. He looked down at the multicoloured synthetic carpet in embarrassment; he had to play his role well. He had to acquire an ally, at least that's what the other man had to believe. He mustn't arouse his antipathy, which would render him unusable. The man named Henrik who was unfaithful had set the rules of the game; he must never know that he had become a helpless pawn in the task Jonas had been assigned.

Jonas raised his eyes and looked at the man who was Eva's.

'I don't quite know how to begin, but I suppose I might as well tell you the plain truth. I'm in love with your wife, and she's in love with me.'

The other man's eyes went blank. Utterly blank. Whatever the man named Henrik had expected, it certainly wasn't the words he had just heard. His mouth fell open, giving his blank stare added support, completing the picture of a man who had totally lost all control of his life. For a long time he stood without uttering a word, and nothing in the world could match the sense of control Jonas felt. Yes – one thing. But he would possess Eva only when he had earned it.

'I understand that this must come as a shock, and I'm terribly sorry to have to do this to you, but somehow I'm sure it's better for you to know what the situation is. I myself have been betrayed once and I know how much it hurts, so I promised myself never to put anyone else through the same thing. I know what betrayal can do to a person.'

The man who was named Henrik and who was unfaithful had closed his mouth now, but the realisation of what this news meant had clearly brought him out of balance. He looked around as if in an attempt to find something appropriate to say.

Jonas fixed his gaze on the man's lips. The lips that had kissed hers, that knew her taste.

He was hiding his clenched fist in his jacket pocket.

'Shouldn't Eva be the one to tell me this?'

'Yes, I know. I tried to talk her into it, but she doesn't dare. She's so afraid of how you'll react. I mean, neither of us wishes you any harm, we really don't, but we can't help the way we feel. We love each other. And of course we have Axel to think of as well.'

The other man's eyes went black when Jonas spoke his son's name.

'For his sake we've tried to break things off several times, but . . . we just can't live without each other.'

That hit home, he could see that. To be able to make choices was one thing, to be rejected quite another.

'Was it Eva who asked you to tell me all this?'

'No, absolutely not.'

There was silence for a moment.

'But I'm doing this for Eva's sake, because I love her. She's the most fantastic woman I've ever met. Perfect in every way. Well, you know what I mean.'

He gave him a confidential smile: just between us studs.

He saw the other man swallow. Now there was clear aversion in his eyes.

'How long have you been seeing each other?'

Jonas pretended to think back.

'It must be about a year now.'

'A year! So you're saying that you and Eva have had a relationship for a year?'

Jonas let the silence speak and saw the impact strike home. Her honour was restored. Now the pig knew that he had cheated on a woman who was loved by another man, someone who deserved her more. Henrik was superfluous in her life. Already rejected.

So. Now you can go. The sooner the better.

'I know. It feels terrible to be duped like this. I wish we'd told you this sooner, so that you could have decided what you wanted to do. It would have been better for all of us if Eva and I had dared to be honest from the start, but we just couldn't do it. This may be poor consolation, but if you only knew how much trouble it is to go behind someone's back. I really want to ask your forgiveness.'

The doors behind them slid open and the blonde woman came in pulling a suitcase on wheels. When she saw them she stopped short and turned indecisively in another direction. When Jonas looked at her, the other man looked too. The man named Henrik who had just learned that nothing was as it seemed picked up his bag.

Jonas couldn't resist asking.

'Is that someone you know?'

'No, but I have to go now.'

He made a move to continue into the terminal, clearly afraid of revealing that the woman was his travelling companion.

Jonas stopped him.

'One more thing, Henrik, for both your sake and mine. Please don't say anything to Eva about this. She told me that you'd be away until Wednesday, and I plan to spend those days trying to convince her to tell you herself when you come back. What more can I do? I hope that in spite of all this you have a pleasant trip. I'll be seeing you.'

With these words he turned and left Henrik to his fate.

He already knew what his own fate would be, and the longing grew stronger with every step as it approached.

In order to endure the waiting, he was going to drive over right now and take a look at her.

When the outer doors to Götgatan 76 slid aside and let her in, it was a quarter past nine. Through the glass of the double doors she saw that the foyer of the Tax Office was already full of people, but she was in no hurry. She had three days to find out what she needed to know; they wouldn't be back until Wednesday.

She had never been here before, but where else than at the Tax Office would it be possible to get hold of someone's tax reference? If she had that, she imagined that everything else would go more smoothly. There was Kerstin's revelation about something troublesome in Linda's past. A piece of information that might be both interesting and useful.

A white notice was taped up on the glass door: 'Please take a number for the desired category.'

Desired category. It was probably better if she didn't say.

There were four alternatives: tax questions, overseas, national registration, birth certificates.

National registration sounded good. She pressed a button for a number slip and sat down on one of the many chairs; there were fifteen numbers ahead of her. She looked around. To her left there were four computers set up, and she got up to take a closer look.

Maybe it was some sort of self-service; it would be best if she didn't have to talk to anyone. One of the computers was free, so she pulled out the chair and sat down. To her left sat a middle-aged man in a checked suit over a sloppily buttoned shirt. Papers spread out on the desk beside him. He looked as if he knew his way around.

'Excuse me.'

He stopped and looked at her.

'If I have a name and address, can I find the social security number on this machine?'

He nodded.

'Go into the main register. Under the start menu.'

'Thanks.'

She followed the instructions and a dialogue box came up with three choices.

Physical woman. Physical man. Legal entity.

Even though 'physical woman' made her furious, she realised that was the category she had to search. She typed in Linda Persson and the address she had given on the day-care list: Duvnäsgatan 14, 116 34 Stockholm.

The computer searched and got a hit.

740317-2402.

Hallelujah. They would be celebrating her birthday during their little love getaway too.

Well, make sure you do celebrate.

She wrote down the number, clicked on Clear and returned to her chair to wait.

'I would like to know where this person was born. Seventy-four, zero three, seventeen, twenty-four, zero two.'

The woman behind the window keyed it into her computer.

'A Linda Persson?'

'Yes.'

'Jönköping.'

The screen was at an angle so she couldn't read it.

'What else does it say?'

'What do you want to know?'

'You couldn't give me a printout, could you?'

'Of course.'

A printer at the woman's side spat out a sheet of paper. Eva accepted it through the open slot in the window. She thanked the woman and got up, reading.

'740317-2402, K, PHOTO (6401 V3.34), Linda Ingrid Persson.'

A bunch of indecipherable abbreviations and then more social security numbers and names. Biological mother and father with complete names and social security numbers and then one more. '670724-3556 Hellström, Stefan Richard. Type S.'

The woman in the window was looking for her next client but Eva got there first.

'Excuse me for asking, but what does "Type S" mean?'

'Spouse.'

A revelation that left her speechless for a moment.

'So you mean this person is married?'

The woman stuck out her hand for the paper and read.

'No, civil status D, divorced since 2001.'

She took in the information, tried to decide what it meant, whether it presented any useful possibilities. They were linked together like one big family, whether those involved liked it or not. Some divorced, some still married.

'Could I get a printout of this social security number as well? Sixty-seven, zero seven, twenty-four, thirty-five, fifty-six.'

The woman typed and another sheet of paper was handed over. Without reading it Eva headed towards the exit.

On the way out through the automatic doors she thought she had received good value for the time spent.

She brewed herself a cup of coffee and even whisked some hot milk into it before she sat down at the desk in his office. He had cleaned up well after himself, not one paper was lying about. She found some notes with scribbled telephone numbers, but since he had left them for her to see she knew they were useless.

Anyway, she no longer needed his help.

She unfolded the paper with the information on Linda's former husband. Residence address in Varberg. Biological parents' names and social security number, the father with a DE, and a new date following the social security number. She picked up the attached sheet with explanations of the abbreviations and saw that it meant Deceased. Under the parents was Linda's name and the S for spouse and the same date for the divorce as on her printout. And then under her, Hellström, Johanna Rebecca. 930428-0318. DE 010715.

A child that had died. The divorce only a few months later. Linda's former husband had lost a child right before they got divorced.

She stood up, feeling bad. The ache in her chest

again, started as always by guilty feelings about Axel. The thought of their inability to give him a good start in life. Wondering whether something might happen to him. How would she be able to survive? She had sometimes wondered whether anyone would dare have a child if they fully understood in advance what it involved. To want the very, very best but always believe that you're not doing enough.

The nervousness and the guilty conscience were a constant companion to the absolutely unconditional love. She was thankful that she hadn't known ahead of time. Axel was the greatest thing in her life; his birth had changed everything, given life new dimensions. She had learned never again to want to put herself in first place, always to be willing to subordinate herself. That is precisely what he had taught her. And yet she spent most of the hours of the day somewhere else, away from him. Despite the fact that over these past six years she'd realised how fast time passed.

And now Henrik intended to see to it that she lost half of what was left. Force her to be an every-other-week mother without giving her the slightest opportunity to choose for herself.

She went to the kitchen and drank some water and then sat down in front of the computer again.

She logged in and clicked onto Google's search site. Searched for Linda's name and got 1,390 hits. She skipped over all the doctoral candidates at the institute of geotechnics and other home pages that definitely had nothing to do with the Linda she was after, but finally had to give up. She added '+Varberg', which gave her information on the results in women's football in division 2 and a complete employee database of the Swedish Municipality Association; neither of those seemed especially relevant. Adding '+Jönköping' produced equally uninteresting results. Linda's ex-husband's name had some hits on lists of results in orienteering competitions, and one hit on a car rental company in Skellefteå, neither of which filled her with much enthusiasm.

She picked up her coffee cup and went into the living room, looking out at the garden through the picture window. How would it feel to keep living here alone with Axel? Would she be able to cope with doing everything herself? And then the next question, more of a realisation: would there actually be any big difference?

Out of the corner of her eye she saw something move in the corner of the yard, close to where the common began. The deer were certainly getting bolder. Soon she would have to start locking the doors to keep them out of the house.

She walked by the dishwasher on her way back and put in her empty coffee cup, then went and sat at the computer again and read one more time the names on the two printouts from the Tax Authority.

Hellström, Johanna Rebecca.

Eight years and three months she had lived.

She had a bright idea and typed in '+Varberg'.

One hit.

Evening News: 'Father accuses ex-wife of daughter's death.'

She raised her eyes and stared out the window in front of her.

Then she returned to the screen and clicked on the link to the article.

A photo of a gravestone and a man standing in front of it with his back to the camera.

Our beloved daughter
*Rebecca Hellström * 1993 † 2001*

And then the caption: 'She's lying.' The father of drowning victim Rebecca Hellström is full of sorrow and bitterness. 'I know that the accident could have been prevented.'

She raised her eyes and stared out the window again. She tried to identify what she was feeling. She had found what she was looking for – no, more than that – but instead of celebrating she was briefly able to take a step back from all the blackness inside her and observe herself sitting in front of the computer. As if a remnant of the old Eva deep inside demanded to make herself heard, tried to warn her.

Think carefully now.

She looked at the screen again.

If you make your bed, you'll have to lie in it.

She got up and went to the kitchen, opened the refrigerator, then closed it again without remembering what she was looking for.

Then she picked up the cordless phone from the kitchen counter and called Enquiries.

'I'm looking for the number of Varberg District Court. Could you please connect me.'

The sound of keys clacking and then the ringing tones.

'Varberg District Court, Marie-Louise Johannesson.'

'Hello, my name is Eva. I'd like to check on the verdict in a trial that took place in November of 2001.'

'What's the case number?'

'I don't know.'

'I'll need that to be able to find the court disposition.'

'How would I find it?'

'What type of case was it?'

'A drowning accident. An eight-year-old girl who drowned, and the woman accused was married to the father.'

'Oh, that one. She was acquitted, I can remember that verdict without a case number.'

'Never mind, then. So she was acquitted?'

'Yes.'

'Thanks a lot.'

She put down the phone on the counter and opened the refrigerator one more time without knowing why, closed it and met Axel's gaze from the photo that was hung up with one of his refrigerator magnets made of magic clay. She remembered that he said it was supposed to be a dinosaur, and it did look like one.

Blue, innocent eyes that believed everything they saw.

Convinced that everyone was good and utterly trusting that they meant what they said. Such as his beloved day-care teacher. Whom he trusted blindly and who looked after his welfare in the daytime but who in actuality was about to destroy his world.

The probability that Henrik was right now planning to make her Axel's new part-time mother effectively slammed the door on the soul-searching that had suddenly overcome her. Never in her life! It wasn't enough that he was going to rob her of half of Axel's childhood without her having the least say in the matter; on top of all that she would be forced to agree to let Axel live every other week under the same roof as *her*. Never! If Henrik intended to live with that woman, then by God she would get sole custody.

Was there any parent who would want to turn over responsibility for their child to such a person? Would the other parents in the day-care group think it was suitable to have a teacher who was accused of causing the death of an eight-year-old because she would rather talk on the phone?

She realised that this was an interesting thought, and something that she ought to explore.

With her gaze fixed on Axel's eyes she made her decision.

Made her choice.

All she had to do was write the name 'Linda' as a note of explanation at the top of the paper when she printed out the article. Then she stuffed it in an anonymous envelope, looked at the day-care list, and addressed it to Simon's already enraged mother.

A year.

The mere thought was like a punch in the stomach. Each time the thought recurred its effect penetrated even deeper. During their holiday last summer when they drove to Italy. During all the dinners together with their friends. When he accompanied her to London on that business trip and they had made love. Both before and after that, that motherfucker had been there. Making him look like a bungler who was completely inadequate. A mediocre husband who could simply be exchanged and replaced by anyone.

He was sitting on the built-in sofa attached to the wall and looking out the porthole of the luxury cabin. The quay at Nyckelviken slipped by, and Nicke and Nocke towered above the horizon like twin exclamation points over all that meant home.

His bag stood unopened on the floor. From the bathroom he could hear her moving about, how her hand kept rummaging at regular intervals amongst all the necessities she had brought along.

A year.

I'm in love with your wife, and she's in love with me.

The bathroom door opened, and she stood expectantly just outside the threshold. He registered that she had on a thin, light-yellow silk dressing gown and that her hair was done in a way he had never seen before.

He returned to the view out the porthole.

For his sake we have tried to break this off several times, but . . . We just can't live without each other.

Out of the corner of his eye he saw her go over to her opened suitcase on the bed.

'Did you call for more towels yet?'

Her tone was brusque and irritated.

He turned his head and looked at her again.

'No.'

It hadn't been a conscious choice. Of course, they had ascertained when they came in that more were needed, but out of well ingrained habit he had waited for her to take the initiative. She was the one who would ring and arrange it.

Just as she always did.

For the first time it struck him with undeniable force how all the years with Eva had marked him. How restful it had been to be able to hide behind her energy. And it suddenly occurred to him how paralysingly threatening it felt to be forced to let go and leave behind everything he was accustomed to. Who was he then, without all that?

'Are you going to do it?'

He fell back to reality from the sting in her voice.

'What?'

'Ring for more towels. Or shall I do it myself?'

'No, I can ring if you like.'

He braced his hands on his thighs as he stood up, went over to the little desk and began listlessly leafing through one of the shipping company's brochures.

Perfect in every way. Well, you know what I mean. What a fucking bastard.

He put down the brochure, no longer sure of what he was looking for, and returned to the porthole. Nicke and Nocke had vanished from the view provided by the thick armoured glass. He closed his eyes in an attempt to conquer the desire to go out on deck and into the fresh air to see whether they were still in sight.

When he turned round she had put the suitcase on the floor and sat curled up on the bed with her back leaning against the veneered headboard. Her nipples were clearly visible under the thin silk gown and signalled that she had taken off her underwear. In her hand she held a tax-free catalogue, but he could see that she wasn't reading it. She had purposefully fixed her gaze on it to emphasise her disappointment over his lack of attention and interest.

At once he realised what was expected of him, but he also knew it was impossible. All the desire that a few hours ago was driving him insane had run out of him like paraffin from a leaky can. What was still flammable had remained on the floor inside the doors of the Viking Line terminal at Stadsgården.

How in hell would he be able to stand a whole day locked in a cabin out on the open sea? Not to mention the hotel visit in picturesque Nådendal which was included in the ticket price for their Romantic Crossing. As soon as they reached the cabin she had already playfully held up two packets of newly purchased Cho-San condoms. 'You can't get any closer than that', as their slogan said.

She was so adamant that they make all the important decisions, plan for the future, finally decide.

But he had suddenly discovered that he didn't know a thing. Not even what alternatives he had to choose from.

With a sudden movement she put down the tax-free catalogue and crossed her arms over her chest in an irritated gesture.

'Don't you feel well?'

Her tone clearly showed that the question was not asked out of concern but as an accusation.

'I suppose I'm all right.'

'Suppose?'

Like a stab, and the acid in her voice was still there.

'What is it then? I thought we were going to make sure we had some fun on this trip.'

In annoyance she tucked back a long blonde ringlet behind her ear and folded her arms across her chest again. The silk gown parted with her movements, showing her cleavage. He noted that it didn't help matters either, but suddenly it felt intolerable not to be able to talk to her about how he felt. He was used to sharing all his thoughts with her. She had been his sanctuary from gloominess. The silver lining. The excitement. The two of them, sharing endless, secret conversations with constantly new, unexplored side-tracks. She always managed to make him feel good, make it worthwhile. The laughter that was so easy to find, her hand that suddenly and unexpectedly touched him where he least expected it, that had *wanted* to touch him.

The way Eva never did.

So many abandoned urges and needs that she had

satisfied when she stormed into his life. Like a dried-up sponge he had soaked up her attention.

Where and when had he and Eva begun to forget? Stopped making an effort and begun to neglect what they had. Once Eva must have been all that he now thought he had found in Linda. Or had she? Had he really ever felt the same way towards her? If so, when did they pass that moment that was the turning point, started moving in reverse? Or perhaps not in reverse, but towards indifference. And if that was the case, had he really arrived at that state of indifference? If he had, how could it be so utterly excruciating to imagine her with another man? Was it merely an escape he had been pursuing? Aside from the disappointment over the fact that she may never have loved him completely and truly, never been filled with dread at the thought of losing him. Merely continued living with him out of duty and consideration. The thought was insufferable. He desperately tried to mobilise a sense of rage to hide behind, but all he found was panic over the fact that everything was starting to crumble, fall apart around him. He looked at Linda and suddenly he wanted her to hold him, understand how much the betrayal hurt, how afraid he was. More than anything else just now, he needed her sympathy.

With a deep sigh he sank down on the built-in sofa again.

'Eva has someone else.'

Her arms that were crossed so tightly over her chest fell to her lap as if they were suddenly liberated from a painful straitjacket. The look of displeasure on her face dissolved in a single breath.

'But Henrik, that's perfect, that solves everything!'

At first he didn't hear what she said. He heard the words, but for the life of him he couldn't understand what they could possibly mean.

Her face radiated true joy. As if she had just opened a package and found what she always wanted but never thought she would receive.

'I mean, we don't have to hide any longer. If she already has someone else, then we all get what we want.'

'But apparently it's been going on for a whole year.'

It was obviously almost too good to be true. She beamed with sheer happiness, having resolved the entire situation in just a couple of sentences.

'This is totally incredible. And here you were feeling so guilty about Axel, for being the one who's breaking up the family. Don't you realise what this means? She's the one, not you, who has made sure there will be a divorce. She was unfaithful even before we met.'

And then to top it off, jubilation at the splendour of life.

'You're finally free!'

And he knew instantly that she would never understand.

And he would never be able to explain it.

There was another man who had stolen his place. A man Eva chose above him, someone she thought was more attractive, more exciting, more intelligent, worth more.

Someone better.

A man who for a whole year had gone around knowing that he was superior to him, had heard things about him and it had all been to his disadvantage, poor Henrik who wasn't good enough, who didn't have anything more to offer. He had been outwitted. That coward had sneaked around behind the scenes of his life without daring to show himself, but all the time he had enjoyed complete insight into and control over Henrik's life. Pulled the strings a bit here and there while Henrik ran around like an idiot, humiliating himself in full view.

His sudden anger demanded that he stand up.

'But don't you get what I'm saying? This isn't about any bloody guilt feelings. She's been going behind my back for a whole fucking year. A whole year! Screwing some fucking toyboy without saying a thing.'

His unexpected emotional outburst made her fall silent in astonishment, and the pause was long enough for him to regret his words. A conflict was the last thing he wanted.

Or dared.

With a furious movement she drew her gown together at the neck.

'And what about you? What have you been doing the past seven months?'

Yes. What could he say? To be quite honest, he no longer had any idea.

'But there's obviously a small difference. I'm at least a fucking twenty-nine-year-old.'

He sank back down on the sofa.

'Stop it.'

'What do you want me to say?'

He had no idea. So he sat in silence, letting the thudding, dull sounds of the motors from the vessel's engine room merge with his confusion.

'Maybe you want me to comfort you in some way?'

I'm in love with your wife, and she's in love with me.

'You have to excuse me, but I just don't feel like it. And to tell you the truth, I don't really understand why there should be any reason, at least not unless you've been lying to me the whole time.'

She got off the bed and put on a jumper from her suitcase. Hasty movements, as if she wanted to get out of there as quickly as he did. As she walked towards the bathroom he saw her run her hand over her left cheek. So much she had believed and hoped. And so much he had wanted and promised. A wave of tenderness passed through him. Above all else he didn't want to hurt her. She deserved a little happiness after all she had been through, but to his amazement he discovered that he wasn't ready for her dreams.

She stopped outside the bathroom door but didn't look at him.

'I'll take the ferry back from Åbo tonight.'

Then she stepped through the doorway and closed the door carefully behind her.

At the day-care centre there was no visible trace of Sunday's meeting. Kerstin had seen to it that everything should be as normal as possible, and she stopped Eva on her way out the door to thank her once again for her efforts, for managing to quell the angry feelings and preventing the meeting from degenerating. And Eva had smiled self-consciously and assured her that she had only done what felt right and proper.

Axel was sitting in the back seat. She hadn't told her parents why she was stopping by. That it wasn't just to have coffee. She hadn't revealed that the real reason was that she needed to borrow some money. A lot of money. And the thought that she would have to tell them all about what was going on, that Henrik was about to leave her for another woman, filled her with deep shame.

'Mamma, look at what I got today.'

She cast a glance in the rear view mirror and saw something brown and red in Axel's hand.

'Oh, how nice. Who gave you that?'

'I don't know his name.'

How was she ever going to admit to her parents that Henrik didn't want her any more, without shattering all their illusions about her. She knew that it would hurt them as much as it did her. Maybe even more. Most of all she didn't want to disappoint them. Not after all they had done for her, all they had managed to give her.

Which she would not be able to give her son.

'Don't you know his name? Is he in one of the other classes?'

'No, he was tall. As tall as you.'

Strange that Linda's substitute would give presents to the children.

'Was he working at the day-care today?'

'No, he was standing outside the fence by the woods and then he called me while I was on the swing and said he was going to give me something nice.'

The car slowed without her being aware that she had put her foot on the brake. She pulled over to the kerb, pulled on the hand-brake and turned to look at him.

'Let me see it!'

He handed her a little brown teddy bear with a red heart on its stomach.

'What else did he say?'

'Nothing special. He said I was good at swinging and that he knew a playground where there were a whole bunch of swings and a slide that was really long and maybe we could drive out there sometime if I wanted and if you said it was OK.'

A tight band was being strapped around her chest. She tried to keep her temper and not raise her voice and frighten him.

'Axel, I told you not to talk to grown-ups that you don't know. And you absolutely must not take anything that any grown-up wants to give you.'

'But he knew my name. Then it doesn't count, right?'

She had to swallow, take a deep breath.

'How old was he? Was he like Pappa or was he more like Grandpa?'

'Like Pappa but maybe not quite as old.'

'How old was he then?'

'Maybe seventy-five.'

'Did any of the teachers see you talking to him?'

'I don't know.'

'What did he look like?'

'I'm not sure. Why do you sound so angry?'

How could she ever explain? The thought that anything might ever happen to him made her stop breathing.

'I'm not angry. I just worry a lot.'

'But he was nice. Why can't I talk to him?'

'Did you recognise him? Have you ever seen him before?'

'I don't think so. But he said maybe he would come by again.'

'Now you have to listen to me carefully, Axel. If he comes by again, I want you to go and get one of the teachers so she can talk to him. Will you promise to do that? You mustn't talk to him alone ever again.'

He sat in silence, picking at the red heart on the bear's stomach.

'Promise me that, Axel.'

'All right!'

She took a deep breath and reached for her phone. All other thoughts were put aside except for the habitual instinct to call Henrik and tell him what had happened. Then in the next moment it struck her that he was on a secret love cruise with their son's day-care teacher and thought he had more urgent activities to devote himself to than worrying about his son. From now on she was alone, she just had to get used to it. She put down the phone and decided to call Kerstin tonight after Axel was asleep and ask them to pay more attention in future. Or she might consider keeping him away from there until they had got hold of the stranger who knew Axel's name.

That problem was solved as soon as she told her parents about the incident. They offered at once to let Axel stay with them for a few days instead. Until they were reassured that the man wouldn't come back.

They were sitting in the kitchen with their coffee cups and a freshly baked sponge cake, and everything could have been just as timeless and secure as it used to be whenever she came back to her childhood home. Instead she now sat with heart pounding, filled with guilt and shame over her own shortcomings.

Axel had sat down by the old, out-of-tune piano in the living room and they could hear him clinking the keys, stubbornly trying to find the right notes to 'Old Man Noah', which she persisted in trying to teach him.

She had to tell them now, while Axel couldn't hear what awaited him. That his pappa would be moving out, that he wouldn't be living at home any more. Time after time she tried, but how could she find the words when she was forced to admit her defeat? That she had been rejected. Dumped. That she was undesirable. Not good enough for her man any more.

She sat there, growing more and more morose the

more Axel figured out 'Old Man Noah', and she knew that time was running out.

'How are things really?'

She met her mother's gaze, realised that she knew something was wrong.

'All right, I suppose.'

There was a brief silence as her parents looked at each other, that look of total understanding that made all words superfluous, a look that she had wanted to be able to share with someone her whole life.

'Now, we don't want to interfere, but if there's something you want to talk about then . . .'

Her father let the sentence die unfinished and put the ball in her court. She felt her hands shaking and wondered if they noticed. Never in her life had she believed that she would ever have a hard time asking them for help, telling them the truth.

She swallowed.

'Maybe things aren't that good after all.'

'No, that's what we thought.'

There was silence again. Soon 'Old Man Noah' would be finished, and every second was precious.

Then with an enormous effort she forced out the words.

'Henrik and I are getting a divorce.'

Her mother and father sat quite calmly, their faces expressionless. But she was having a hard time remaining in her chair. For the first time she had given voice to the words and felt them penetrate her from outside. She had sent them straight out into the universe like a fact that could not be called back. For the first time their import became real. She was one of those who had failed, who had made her son a child of divorce.

'So, it's that bad.'

Her father had a worried furrow in his brow.

His words confused her. Why weren't they surprised? What had they seen that she couldn't see?

Her mother interpreted her reaction, as usual, but it was with sorrow in her voice that she began to explain.

'Well, we might as well be honest. It's like this: from the beginning we thought that you and Henrik were a little too, what should I say, a little too different perhaps. But you were so sure and wanted him so much, so what could we say? And what right did we have to meddle in your choice of a husband? You've always done what you wanted, after all.'

She lovingly placed her hand on Eva's and smiled.

'We could see how you two were getting along, and we worried that you would tire of each other in the long run. We didn't think he would be able to live up to all the expectations we knew you had. That's not to say that I'm particularly glad that we were right.'

Eva pulled her hand away, afraid that her mother would feel it shaking. Everything in chaos. She looked around the kitchen, let her gaze rest on the old glass tray on the wall that came from her great-grandmother's house. Generations of hard-working couples who through their struggles had given her opportunities and led her to this. One generation follows another. Until she came and broke the chain with her failure. The Great Loser who wasn't good enough for her husband and who would mark her son and the rest of the generational chain and pass down new values for what love and marriage were. Something deceitful and unreliable. Not worth fighting for, or believing in at all.

Her father put down his coffee cup with a familiar clatter of home.

'How's Henrik taking it? He must be very upset.'

She looked at her mother, dumbfounded. And then at her father, still so proud of his daughter who took command of her own life, who wouldn't settle for less than the best, who was worth so much more.

And an iron curtain dropped in front of the truth.

'Well . . . he's doing OK, I suppose.'

'What have you decided to do about the house?'

Be careful what you say now.

Weak and powerless, the voice from inside the dark tried to make itself heard one last time.

If you make your bed you have to lie in it.

Then she turned her head and looked at her father and the voice from the Eva who once existed gave up and fell silent, unable to warn her again.

And inside herself she prayed to be allowed to meet, for once in her life, someone who would stand by her side and love her, someone she could lean on when she no longer had the strength to fight.

'I'm going to buy Henrik out and keep the house. I'm going to need to borrow some money.'

Horrid was the word he thought could best describe the remainder of their crossing, even if it was an understatement. The Baltic Sea was smooth as a mirror, but the calm outside was amply compensated for by the tornado that struck him, that tore loose every feeling he thought was firmly anchored in a decision taken. Everything he had known, wanted, dreamed. It was all one big mess.

The longest half-hour of his life she had spent locked in the bathroom before she burst out, packed her things in a rage and without saying a word slammed the door of their luxury cabin behind her.

He had remained sitting where he was, looking out the porthole as the archipelago thinned out and Stockholm and home vanished farther and farther out of reach. After a few hours he made his way down to the lobby and changed his return trip reservation to that same night. She had done the same, he learned. He had no idea where she was during the rest of the crossing.

In Åbo he had changed ferries; as sheer punishment he was given a windowless cabin on a lower deck below the water level, and that's where he had continued his isolation. Just after midnight there was an urgent knock on his door. She was drunk. Furiously she screamed at him, using all the obscene words he could remember ever hearing, and when he didn't defend himself the air went out of her. In tears she collapsed on the floor inside the cabin door. But he was unable to console her. For the life of him he couldn't come up with anything to say. And when she realised his total inability to handle all that had happened, her wrath was reawakened and with a new onslaught of vituperation she left the cabin, slamming the door, leaving him to the confined space with her words hanging in the air. And he realised that he deserved every one of them. He remained sitting among them and spent the next few hours in soul-searching until he could stand it no longer. Because he had been betrayed as well. A judge ought to come down on his side, weighing the punishment he deserved for what he had done to Linda against the sympathy to which he was entitled after Eva's betrayal.

It would have been so much easier if everything were black or white. The tightrope he would have been forced to walk with a furious need to accuse her without any of his own guilt. Silence her with her guilty conscience and rob her of every possibility of defending herself. Force her to admit her wretchedness and thereby finally take the power from her. Gain superiority over her.

Instead he would obsequiously have to attempt to win back her love, persuade her in an ingratiating way, try to convince her to stay with him. Choose his words well and not give her the slightest opportunity of minimising her crime by dumping part of the guilt onto him, by saying that he had behaved no better himself.

* * *

It would have been so much easier if he had told her the truth from the beginning. If he had confessed his secret love or passion or whatever it was he felt or had felt. Then they could have continued from the point they were at now, with all their cards on the table. Now it was too late. Now his admission that he had lied cast him into the underworld and from there he could never become her equal. Even if she had done the same thing to him, her verbal prowess would quickly shift all right and truth to her side.

There was something about Eva that made him feel superfluous. She was so unbelievably strong. Adversity seemed to have the opposite effect on her that it did on other people. She didn't react normally. For her adversity was a reason, and fuel to become even stronger. In some unfathomable way she always managed to convert a crisis into an opportunity. As he stood by and kept silent and realised that she didn't need him, that she could solve everything on her own with no need for his help or support. Bit by bit she had stripped him of all responsibility until finally he hadn't known whether he could handle anything at all. Good God, he wasn't even allowed to open his own window envelopes!

With Linda everything had been different. She had openly admitted that she needed him; it was a fantastic feeling to be indispensable. She made him feel like a man. Straight off she admitted that there were things that she couldn't do or hadn't mastered, and unlike Eva there was nothing shameful in it for her. On the contrary, she used it to come closer to him, to make them dependent on each other, to help them create an essential togetherness. And he had enjoyed their solidarity. He had fantasised about their life together and how different everything would be. How different *he* would be. Now he realised how naïve he had been, how simple everything had seemed as long as it was merely a fantasy. He had imagined that he would be able to cut Eva out of his life and his future like an old wart he finally got around to doing something about. That everything would be clean and pure and full of possibilities. An unblemished new start, completely unaffected by everything that had gone before, all the choices he had once made. He realised now with devastating clarity that it could never be that way; he and Eva belonged together forever, whether they wanted it or not. The choices he had already made would follow him for the rest of his life. Axel was one of the consequences. He had only seen the advantages, forgotten to imagine Eva and Axel together with a new man, a man who would spend as much time with Axel as he did. Influence him and the grown man he would one day become. Now that he had got a look at that bastard, the thought was intolerable.

But the thought of losing Linda was intolerable as well.

Or of being rejected by Eva.

Or that she may never have loved him.

Bloody hell.

He needed time. Time to understand what it was he actually felt.

What it was he actually wanted.

He got up and found the key card. He had to try and get hold of Linda. Whether it was out of consideration or because the walls of the cabin were threatening to suffocate him, he didn't know. He got her cabin number from the reception, but there was no answer when he knocked. No one was answering her phone either. Methodically he searched through the bars and restaurants on board. What was it he wanted from her? He didn't know. All he knew was that he had to talk to her. Try to make her understand. She wasn't on any of the flashing disco floors or in the loud karaoke bars. He stopped in front of a large panoramic window, having lost his orientation, and in all the pitch blackness outside the window it was impossible to discern the direction they were sailing, whether he was closer to the bow or the stern. He found a wall map and made his way back to her cabin. This time she opened the door, squinting at the sharp light in the corridor. She didn't say a word, just left the cabin door open and backed into the darkness inside. He took a deep breath before he followed her, still not knowing what he wanted to say. Then he closed the door behind him and stood there in the dark.

'Don't turn on the light.'

He heard her voice a few metres away and pulled back his hand that had automatically been searching the wall for a light switch.

'I can't see a thing.'

She didn't answer. He heard the sound of a glass being set down on a table. A faint light from the porthole began to materialise and then the contours of a chair. He stood there trying to let his eyes adjust. Didn't want to risk tripping over something on the floor. But he had to figure out what to say.

'How are you feeling?'

She didn't answer this time either. Only a faint snort broke through the throbbing engine noise.

He stood in silence a long time. The initiative was his but he didn't know what to say, what words he could use to make her understand.

'Do you have anything to drink?'

'No.'

He heard her pick up the glass and take a few gulps. This was not going to be easy.

'Linda, I . . .'

He had palpitations now. He felt so much and could explain none of it. She who had been his closest friend. Who had understood him so well. Who had made him feel so good. Who had made him dare.

He heard her change position. Maybe she was sitting up.

'What do you want?'

Four words.

Each by itself or in some other context completely harmless. Utterly without gravity in themselves. Merely a question about what he wanted.

But at this moment the words coming from her lips were a threat to his entire existence. Now he would be forced to make the choice he would have to live with for the rest of his life. Open the way towards the future he would freely choose, here and now. Now he had a chance. Or did he? That was precisely what he didn't know any longer, whether he actually had any other choice. And that's what made it all so hard. He no longer knew. Maybe this was the only alternative. Maybe the decision had already been made, over his head.

By Eva.

Again.

Shit.

Surely Linda realised that everything had changed, didn't she? That it wasn't so easy any more? She couldn't ask him to make such a big decision without giving him a chance to think or figure out what was going on.

'If you still don't have anything to say then you might as well leave.'

There was a coldness in her voice that scared him. He was on his way to losing everything. Both what he had and what he dreamed of having. Both. What would he do then? If he was left all alone.

'Please, can't we just turn on the light so I can see you?'

'Why should you see me? It doesn't seem to be anything you want.'

He felt the rage building. It was such a shame for her! She was lying there so pitiful and refused to make the slightest effort to try and understand or meet him halfway.

She was the one who spoke.

'I just want to hear your answer to my question. That's all I ask and it doesn't matter if it's in the dark. What is it you want, anyway?'

He could see her contours now. She was sitting up in bed. A single cabin the same as his.

'It's not that fucking simple!'

'What isn't simple?'

'Everything has changed.'

'What has changed?'

Now he could also make out the floor, and he went

over to the chair, picked up her jacket that was hanging over the back and placed it in his lap as he sat down.

He gave a heavy sigh.

'I don't know how to explain.'

'Try.'

Shit.

Shit, shit, shit.

'It's not as if my feelings for you have changed, that's not it.'

She sat in silence. It was harder to make out her contours from this angle. Maybe it was true that it was easier to say what he had to say without being able to see her.

'It just feels like . . . I know it sounds strange, but . . . Eva and I lived together for almost fifteen years. Even though I don't love her . . . I just can't fathom that she has been with another man for a whole year. Without saying a word. I just feel so stupid.'

The darkness was working in his favour. He didn't need to see her or show his shame. And he didn't want her questions and accusations. He wanted her support. Her understanding.

'I've never told you about this. I don't think I've ever told anyone, not even Eva. It's a long time ago now, back in Katrineholm before I moved to Stockholm.'

A girl he had loved. Unconditionally and to distraction. At least he had thought so. Twenty years ago, with no frame of reference. Everything new and untested. Untried. No limits.

'There was a girl there, Maria was her name. She was a year younger than me. We moved in together in a little bed-sit in the city right after high school. I was really in love with her . . .'

The price had been high. He had risked everything but not for a second had he felt secure. It had been a crazy balancing act from the beginning; he had loved her more than she did him. Every waking moment was a struggle to regain balance. Every day a paralysing fear of losing her, a fear that in the end controlled his whole life. And he had good reason to be afraid. He never succeeded in trusting her, in spite of her protestations that everything was as it should be. She had lulled him into a false sense of security which he finally had to believe in because he had no other choice. Until his suspicions had been confirmed by the testimony of others.

'She went behind my back. I had a suspicion about it the whole time, but she assured me that it wasn't true. But in the end she admitted that she had met someone else.'

Never again will anyone do me so wrong. Never be able to fool me like that. I will never again let anyone all the way in.

Twenty years later and the wound was still there. He had kept his promise. Until he met Linda. She had forced him to dare.

Now Eva had sabotaged everything by picking the wound open again.

He heard her drinking from the glass. Sensed her movements as shadows in the dark.

'I have only one question. What is it you want?'

He closed his eyes. Gave an honest answer.

'I don't know.'

'Then I want you to leave.'

'Linda, please.'

'I know what I want, I've known it for a long time,

and I've told you about it. You told me what you wanted too, but I realise now that you didn't mean a word of it.'

'Yes I did.'

'You most certainly did not!'

'Yes I did, it's just that everything is different now.'

'Well, so be it. Then there wasn't any more to it than that. You find out that your wife is doing it with someone else and suddenly we don't mean shit any more. Bloody hell!'

She lay back on the bed again.

'Linda, that's not what this is about.'

'Then what is it that has changed so much? If it's not your feelings for me? Just a few days ago we went and looked at a flat together!'

Give me a year on a desert island.

With all my choices intact.

'Can't you wait for me?'

'Wait for what? For you to see if you can get her back?'

'No!'

'What am I supposed to wait for, then? For you to make up your mind whether I'm good enough as a replacement?'

'Cut it out, Linda. I just feel that everything's moving too fast. I do realise that because I'm reacting this way that . . . that . . .'

He broke off. What was it he had actually realised?

'That you actually love your wife?'

'No, that's not true. I really don't.'

Or did he?

'It's not that. I just realise that . . . that I'm not ready yet . . . it wouldn't be fair to you to . . .'

Please, get me out of this!

'I'm just not ready. It wouldn't be fair to you if we started a life together when I'm feeling this way.'

'So you think I should sit and wait for you? In case you ever happen to be ready?'

'Everything is so much easier for you! You're not risking anything.'

She sat up again.

'I'm not risking anything! I'm a day-care teacher who's having an affair with the father of one of the children! What do you think will happen to me when this gets out? And those emails that somebody sent? How do you think it feels to have someone go into my computer and find my private letters and then send them off? Don't you get it? Somebody knows. Somebody who has seen us. Who's trying to punish me!'

'It wasn't Eva. I know you think so, but she's not like that. And why in hell would she do it? She must be satisfied by now. It gives her a free hand, after all.'

Linda was silent, and he saw that she was shaking her head, slowly shaking it back and forth in disgust.

At him.

'Listen to yourself. Listen to what you're saying. Poor little rejected Henrik. It's such a fucking shame!'

He didn't reply.

He had lost her.

She went over and opened the cabin door. The sharp glare from the fluorescent lights in the hallway blinded him. All that was left of her was a black silhouette.

'You're never going to be ready, Henrik. If I were you I'd spend my time finding out who I am and what I actually want to do with my life. Then you can go out and involve others in your future.'

He swallowed. The lump in his throat wouldn't go away.

'Now go.'

He couldn't recall the last time he had felt so nervous. The enormous bouquet of roses on the seat next to him suddenly looked grotesque, like a foolish prop in an even more foolish film. It was just after ten in the morning, and he was grateful that he would have the day alone at home so he could collect himself before she came home from work. He hadn't called to tell her that he was returning a day early.

He was close now. Close to home. But he had never felt so far away. He cursed at a badly parked old Mazda that stood halfway out in the road just before the right turn into his street. With one hand on the wheel he manoeuvred his way past and in the next moment he saw his house.

Her car was in the driveway.

Why wasn't she at work?

And then the next thought.

Maybe she wasn't alone inside. Maybe she had made sure to bring home her lover now that Henrik was out of the way for a few days, show him their home, what she had to offer in the way of material assets. The thought disgusted him as much as it scared him. He stood alone now while there were two of them. And he was the one who would have to leave the house, she was the one who had the financial wherewithal to buy him out. And then that other bastard would move into his house, get to enjoy all the hard work he had done to fix it up. Fuck. And she who had been so understanding. Suggested maybe he should go away for a few days and think. I'll take care of everything here at home in the meantime, it's quite all right, the main thing is that you feel good again. I'm here if you need me, I always will be. Maybe I've been poor at showing it, but I'll try to improve.

How was it possible to be so cold and calculating, all to get rid of him for a few days so she could fuck her lover in peace. Who was she really, this woman he had lived with for almost fifteen years? Did he know her at all?

And the trip she had paid for. And the champagne. Had it all been to assuage her guilty conscience?

He opened the car door, took the bouquet of roses and climbed out. If she had seen him through a window he couldn't very well retreat now. But what would he do if the other man was in the house?

He took his time after he put the key in the door. Made as much noise as possible to give them time to interrupt whatever they were doing. A bedroom drama was the last thing he wanted to deal with right now. He put his bag down on the hall floor and looked around for strange shoes or coats without finding any.

Her voice from upstairs.

'Hello?'

Instinctively he hid the bouquet behind his back.

'It's only me.'

Her steps across the floor upstairs and then her feet, legs and finally all of her visible halfway down the stairs, where she stopped. The expression on her face was hard to read, maybe surprised, maybe annoyed.

'I thought you weren't coming back until tomorrow night.'

'No, I know. I changed my mind.'

He swallowed his impulse to ask if she was lonely, his need to know.

They stood there looking at each other, neither of them ready to take the next step. The bouquet burned in his hand, suddenly so embarrassing that he wanted to back out and toss it away before it was discovered.

It was impossible to determine what he actually felt when he saw her. Only a desire to be able to go up the stairs in peace and quiet, sink down in their sofa and let everything be normal. Decide who was going to pick up Axel at day-care, where he would be able to drive without having a stomach ache, and then eat a normal Tuesday dinner together. Ask how Axel was doing, whether anyone had called and where she had put his mail and whether they should rent a movie that evening. But there was a mountain between them. And how he was going to get over that mountain he had no idea. Even less what might be waiting for him on the other side.

'Why aren't you at work?'

He hadn't meant to sound like he was snooping, but he could hear that it sounded like an accusation. And it was more than clear that she was searching for a suitable answer, since she didn't really have one.

'My throat is a little sore.'

She said it on her way back up the stairs, without looking at him. And he knew she was lying. When she was gone he put down the bouquet and quickly took off his jacket, looked at himself in the hall mirror and ran his fingers through his hair. He couldn't remember the last time he had bought her flowers, or whether he had ever done so before. But if he were to be successful with what he had decided to do, then he would have to try and overcome the distaste he felt. He had one single goal, but his feelings were fighting for space inside of him. Anger, fear, confusion, decisiveness.

He took the bouquet and went up the stairs.

She was standing by the kitchen table stacking up sheets of paper. A calculator and a pen. The folder they got from the real estate agent where she put all the bills and loan papers related to the house.

The fear again. Stronger than the anger.

'What are you doing?'

She didn't have time to answer. She looked up at him and saw the blood-red bouquet. Stood there mute and stared at it as if she were trying to identify what it signified. And then, finally, after an uncomfortable pause when all he felt was his own heart pounding, she finally managed to grasp what the bouquet was.

'Did someone send you flowers?'

'No, they're for you.'

He held the bouquet out to her but she didn't move. Not a hint of a reaction. Everything felt hollow. Not a move to step forward and take them. Her indifference made him suddenly feel so embarrassed that it was too much for him, and he wanted to scream out all his accusations right in her face. Crush that false mask devoid of feeling that she hid behind and force her down on her knees. Make her confess. But he had to be smarter than that to manage all this.

He swallowed.

'Shall I put them in water?'

His words got her moving, and she went to the cupboard over the refrigerator where she kept the vases, hesitated briefly when she couldn't reach them, and went back to the kitchen table to get a chair. She didn't say thank you when he handed her the bouquet. Didn't look at him either. Just took the flowers from his hands, turned and went to the sink. He stood looking at her back as she slowly and carefully clipped the ends off the roses and arranged them one by one in the vase.

Perhaps she had already made her decision and stood there preparing herself. Perhaps she would turn around soon and tell him the truth, that she had made up her mind while he was gone. Admit that she had met another man and wanted to live with him instead. He had to forestall her, make her understand that he was ready to fight for what they had, that he would change if she just gave him a chance. He had to make her understand that her decision was based on false assumptions.

He suddenly felt like crying, going over and throwing his arms around her. Stand close behind her and tell her the truth. Once and for all get rid of all the lies and, with them out of the way, be able to feel close to her again. When had they stopped talking to each other? Had they ever been able to talk the way he and Linda had done? Why had it been so easy with her and not with Eva? They had known each other for fifteen years, after all. She knew more about him than anyone else. He couldn't stand not having her friendship any more. They shared far too many memories. And they shared Axel.

Dear Eva. I'm sorry. Forgive me.

It didn't happen. It was a superhuman task to give voice to the words, to admit his infidelity and his lies even though she was no better herself. He refused to expose himself that way, or at least he didn't intend to do it before he had some idea how she would react, whether she intended to reject him or not. But he had to try to approach her, he was in a hurry now, he had to try to reach her before it was too late. Before she turned around and announced her decision.

'I've missed you.'

She didn't turn around but her hand stopped halfway between the sink and the vase.

He could hear how strange the words sounded. As if even the room were reacting. It was so long since anything like that had been said within these walls, and he wondered whether what he said was true. Was it longing for her he had felt? In the strict sense of the word. Yes, it was. The longing for her loyalty.

'I've been thinking while I was away, as you told me to do, and I would like to beg your forgiveness for being so disagreeable lately. And then I got to thinking of that trip you booked to Iceland. I would very much like it if we went on it together.'

Her hand was once again moving between the sink and the vase.

'I cancelled it.'

'We can book another one. *I* can do it.'

Eager, bordering on desperation. A wild attempt to break through, get a first response that would point out what way they were heading. And he hated the fact that he was once again subject to her will, her decision. In a second he was re-acclimatised and robbed of the ability to take action, which he had discovered was something he could do over the past six months.

The phone rang. She reached it first even though he was closer. He had hesitated because he thought they should let it ring.

'Eva.'

She gave him a quick look when she heard who it was. As if she was close to being exposed.

'I haven't got to it yet, can I call you a little later?'

Hadn't got to what?

'Good, I'll do that. See you later.'

She hung up and put down the phone.

'Who was that?'

'Pappa.'

She was lying without looking at him again. It was him – the other man.

Somehow he had to rise up from his position at the bottom. He was the one who had been unpleasant lately. She could continue in peace and quiet to hide behind what was right – wounded and unapproachable, forcing him to make up with her. Somehow he had to get her to confess. But not by accusing her. Then she would only be on her guard and also have a legitimate reason to strike back. No, he had to get her to reveal herself.

She had returned to the roses, although they were all standing as if to attention in the vase.

He decided to try a long shot. It should produce some kind of reaction.

'Janne says to say hello, by the way.'

'Mm-hmm. How are they doing these days?'

'They're fine. He said he saw you at some lunch place a while back.'

'Oh, he did?'

'You didn't seem to see him. He joked and wondered what sort of lamb meat you were out to lunch with.'

With the vase all arranged in her hands, she turned round.

'Lamb meat?'

'Yes, there was some young man you were eating with.'

'I don't remember that, when did he say it was?'

She walked towards the living room with the vase. He followed her.

'A week or so ago, maybe. I'm not sure.'

'It couldn't have been me. He must be mistaken.'

Cool as a cucumber. He didn't know her at all. Had she always been able to lie this easily? Maybe it wasn't the first time she had an affair behind his back; she had had plenty of opportunity over the years. All these business trips and all the overtime she worked. Even if she hadn't eaten lunch with him, the words 'lamb meat' should have bothered her, since her lover was a decade younger than she was.

He felt the anger taking over, and soon he would no longer be able to stop himself before he let it loose. She had set down the vase on the coffee table and now stood straightening up the roses as if they were going to be entered in a symmetry competition.

He turned and headed for the bathroom, feeling a great need to take a shower and wash off everything that had clung to him in the past day.

He checked the bathroom cabinet. No forgotten toothpaste. The wastebasket had been recently emptied and lined with a new plastic bag. There was washing in the machine, and he opened the lid to hang it up. Axel's dark-blue sweatsuit, Eva's black pullover. And then a pair of black lace panties that he had never seen before. He held them up between thumb and fore-finger, disgusted at the thought of . . . God. So that's the way she dressed when she was out with her lover. She had certainly never dressed like that for him.

He took two clothes-pegs and hung the panties up in the drying cabinet so that they would be the first thing she saw when she came into the bathroom, would know that he had discovered them. And start to worry why he didn't comment on them.

He went back upstairs and into the bedroom. The bed was made and the bedspread in place. How could he ever sleep in that bed again?

He pulled out the top drawer in the chest of drawers where she kept her underwear, searched among the sensible panties that he usually saw her wearing. Then to the left, among her bras, another unknown piece of paraphernalia. A black lace bra with padding that he had never seen before. He heard her clattering in the kitchen, held up the bra, and was assaulted by the image of her and the other man together in the double bed behind him, how his feverish hands managed to undo the little clasp he saw before him and expose her breasts. He resisted the impulse to rush out to the kitchen and throw it right in her self-pitying face, forced himself to take a few deep breaths. He was just about to push the drawer back in when he caught sight of something else. A corner of something red. A diary with a lock but with the key hanging on a silver thread from the little heart-shaped lock. A diary? Since when had she spent time on something like that? The sounds from the kitchen assured him that she was still out there. He quickly opened the lock with the little key and started to page through the diary. Blank and not written in. Not a word on the white pages. He was just about to lock it again when something fell into his hand and he discovered hand-written words on the inside of the cover.

'To my Beloved! I am with you. Everything will be fine. A book to fill with memories of all the wonderful things that await us.'

Then he looked down at his palm and didn't want to believe what he saw.

Disgusting, and tied with a light-blue thread, was a light-blond lock of that bastard's hair.

Almost thirteen thousand kronor per month. Just in living expenses. The papers lay in piles spread out on the kitchen table in front of her: mortgage, electric bills, insurance. She could handle the operating costs and the mortgage herself, but she would have to change her habits radically. A cheaper company car. Buy wholesale at discount stores. Write precise shopping lists and buy economy size.

She looked at the folder the real estate agent had given them when they bought the house. A colour picture of a smiling house on the cover. A dark spot right above the chimney. Henrik had spilled his wine when they celebrated the occasion at the Café Opera's sidewalk restaurant on the way home.

Eight years ago.

Her father had asked her to call a surveyor to ascertain the value of the house, and then she could figure out how much she would have to borrow. She would certainly see to it that all the papers were in order the day her husband finally dared to confess his betrayal. In an hour she would be able to withdraw the money and tell him to go to hell.

Suddenly she thought she heard the sound of a key in the door. He wasn't supposed to come home until the following day, so she must be hearing things. It occurred to her that this had happened often in the past few days, that she heard sounds she didn't recognise. Last night when she was in the shower she could have sworn that she'd heard someone upstairs. The balcony door was open and for a moment she had been afraid. Pulled her robe tight around her and went upstairs, looking through all the rooms and the cupboards too, to make sure the house was empty. Axel was staying with her parents, so it wasn't him. For the first time she had a chance to feel what it would be like in the future. Alone in the house. Fear of the dark would upset her. And the other evening she was so sure that someone was standing on the balcony looking at her through the dark windowpane. She had to conquer the fear that was trying to ensnare her, she had to be strong.

Then she heard the sound of the front door opening. Someone came into the hallway.

'Hello?'

'It's only me.'

Henrik. Why in hell was he home early?

There could only be one explanation. He had decided to confess and couldn't contain himself a minute longer so he could relieve his guilty conscience. Now here he came, running home a day early and she hadn't managed to finish everything. She had put the magazine article about Linda in Simon's mother's mailbox yesterday, she must have read it by now, but she hadn't yet heard any reaction from the day-care centre. No urgent call to set up another crisis meeting. And it would be two days from now before she could take out the money she would toss in his face.

He couldn't tell her before that!

She got up and went towards the stairs. She had to collect herself and appear normal, like the understanding housewife she was. Ask him how he was, if he was feeling well, seem glad that he was home early. Not make it easy for him to blurt out what he intended to tell her.

Halfway down the stairs she saw it, even though he was hiding it behind his back, and all her intentions toppled like bowling pins. How could he be so tasteless? He had never bought flowers for her before. Now, of all times, he came home dragging red roses, now that he was going to confess that he had been unfaithful, that he wanted a divorce. What the hell was going on inside that head of his anyway? Did he expect her to be happy? Did he think a bunch of bloody roses would justify his betrayal and make her forgive him? I see, you have a relationship with our son's day-care teacher and want a divorce, so that's it. Awfully sweet of you to finally buy me a few flowers.

She took a deep breath.

'I thought you weren't coming back until tomorrow night.'

'No, I know. I changed my mind.'

She could see how nervous he was. A foolish smile flitted across his face.

Damn it, you could at least take off your jacket.

'Why aren't you at work?'

Because I called in sick and now I'm spending my days sabotaging your future. Just the way you sabotaged mine.

'My throat is a little sore.'

She went back upstairs. Continued on to the kitchen table and started gathering up the papers. She didn't manage to put away everything before he appeared in the room.

'What are you doing?'

There was fear in his voice. The anger she had got used to encountering seemed blown away. Confused, she realised that the Henrik she knew, the one she had lived with for fifteen years but who had been unapproachable lately, was back. He was standing here in the middle of the kitchen trying to reach her.

She looked up at him. A scared little boy with a bouquet of flowers that was much too big held out in front of him. So pitiful, so utterly helpless.

But one thing she knew for sure, even though many other things were confused just now, she definitely didn't want his flowers.

'Did someone send you flowers?'

'No, they're for you.'

He held the bouquet out to her. Accepting the flowers would signal a defeat, a tiny opening for an approach, which she certainly did not intend to give him. She could see that her hesitation annoyed him; for some reason he was doing all he could to appear friendly. She wondered what his plan was. Were they supposed to make up and be good friends again and then he would drop the bomb?

She wasn't going to make it that easy for him.

'Shall I put them in water?'

She realised that she had no choice. That she would be acting far too disagreeably and would help him out by not accepting them.

She took down a vase and went over to him – saying thank you was beyond her. She took the bouquet and turned to the sink. Carefully she clipped off the ends of one rose after another and put them in the vase. He was still standing behind her; maybe he was preparing himself to disclose his confession. She had to stall him, only one more day, just until Linda's past was revealed and she had a chance to get hold of the money. Her unresponsive behaviour would naturally strengthen his resolve that he was doing the right thing by leaving her, but that no longer mattered. So many times she had pursued him through the house in the past six months to get a conversation going. Now it was his turn to pursue her. And then neither of them would pursue the other. Ever. Not in this house or anywhere else.

'I've missed you.'

Her hand stopped halfway between the sink and the vase. Of its own accord. As if just like the rest of her it didn't understand at first what the words signified.

And then all at once she understood what this was all about.

The fear in his voice. The red roses. His silly but valiant attempt at reconciliation.

Something had happened during their trip.

Linda had left him and now he stood here terror-stricken, wanting his wife back. Not because he loved her, but because he had nothing else. That's why he came home early. He and Linda had split up. That's why she suddenly recognised him again, now that the strength he had gained from Linda's infatuation had left him.

'I've been thinking while I was away, as you told me to do, and I would like to beg your forgiveness for being so disagreeable lately. And then I got to thinking of that trip you booked to Iceland. I would very much like it if we went on it together.'

The new conditions set the ground rocking beneath her. She needed time to understand what this meant, how she should handle the situation.

'I cancelled it.'

'We can book another one. *I* can do it.'

He sounded almost desperate now, pleading. He'd do anything if she would only let him back in. And all at once she was forced to admit what she had managed to avoid thinking about. There had been something attractive about his attempt to free himself from her. Not his betrayal and his lies – for those she despised him more than she could describe – but because for the first time he had done something on his own, something that challenged her and her control over him. He had acted like a man, even if he had been a cowardly bastard. He had stopped being another child she had to take care of. And as she put the next rose in the vase she realised that the hatred and desire for revenge aroused by his infidelity was a reaction to the fact that she had actually seen something in him that she could look up to and respect.

His own will.

And now she could have him back.

But it was the old Henrik who stood here now, the Henrik she was used to. She had never in all these years permitted herself to question their relationship – a commitment was a commitment. She had never allowed herself to admit the contempt she felt for his weakness, that he let her control him. With his betrayal he had opened her eyes, and there was no turning back. He had degraded and deceived her; now he had suddenly changed his mind and wanted to come back.

She was the one who would have to make the decision.

And bear the blame forever.

The phone rang. She went over to it and answered, thankful for the respite.

'Eva.'

'Hi, I just wanted to see whether you'd got hold of the surveyor yet.'

She glanced quickly at Henrik, wondering whether he could hear what her father was saying.

He stood with his arms crossed, watching her intently. She couldn't tell if he could hear anything.

'I haven't got to it yet, can I call you a little later?'

'Sure.'

'Good, I'll do that. See you later.'

She hung up and put down the phone.

'Who was that?'

'Pappa.'

He was satisfied with that. Didn't ask what he wanted.

She went back to the roses although they were already arranged in the vase; she had to have something to do to maintain the distance between them.

'Janne says to say hello, by the way.'

She landed gratefully in this neutral topic of conversation.

'Mm-hmm. How are they doing these days?'

'They're fine. He said he saw you at some lunch place a while back.'

'Oh, he did?'

'You didn't seem to see him. He joked and wondered what sort of lamb meat you were out to lunch with.'

She picked up the vase and headed for the living room.

'Lamb meat?'

'Yes, you were eating lunch with some young man.'

'I don't remember that, when did he say it was?'

As far as she could recall, she hadn't eaten lunch with anyone but her colleagues in a very long time. And they were definitely not lamb meat.

'A week or so ago, maybe. I'm not sure.'

He had followed her into the living room.

'It couldn't have been me. He must be mistaken.'

He stood there a second in silence, and she pretended to arrange the bloody roses one more time. Then he finally left; she could hear his steps going down the stairs.

Her gaze fell on one of Axel's toy cars, and she suddenly remembered that she forgot to tell him about the man at day-care, that Axel had spent the night and all day at her parents' house. And she also realised that she had to be the one to pick him up; she had to keep Henrik away from her parents. At least until everything was ready. After that it wouldn't matter.

The living room was warm and smelled stuffy; the sun was shining in and she opened the balcony door a bit before she went back to the kitchen and opened the dishwasher. Another task to hide behind for a while. She heard him come up the stairs, saw him out of the corner of her eye as he walked past the doorway and noticed with gratitude that he kept going towards the bedroom.

The confusion she felt was so complete that she had a hard time remembering where the china she was taking out of the dishwasher was supposed to go. She had thought she was in full control over events, but now all her assumptions had changed, all the bits of the puzzle had been tossed up in the air and had fallen in disarray. She would have to back up a few steps in her plan of action to regain control. What consequences would the article she had put in Simon's mother's mailbox have now? She no longer knew. She didn't give a damn what happened to Linda, but perhaps her own actions would now work against her plan. She needed time to think.

She saw Henrik pass by the kitchen doorway again, on his way from the bedroom. This time without even looking at her. If she lay down on the bed and pretended to take a nap, she would have time to think in peace and quiet. She had stayed home from work because she had a sore throat, after all.

She went into the bedroom and closed the door behind her. There was a red book lying on the bedspread with a little padlock on the side. And her black lace bra that she had humiliated herself by buying in another life. She sank down on the bed. What did he mean by this? Hadn't he crossed the line now? She quickly put the bra back in the top drawer, couldn't bear to look at it. Then she sat down on the bed again, took the book and weighed it in her hand. He knew quite well that she didn't keep a diary, so why in the world had he bought this one? She unhooked the little padlock and opened the first page. Something fell out and landed in her lap. At first she didn't see what it was, and when she did she couldn't believe it was true. Once again it was clear that she didn't know the man she had lived with for fifteen years. The Henrik she thought she knew would never in his life think of cutting off a lock of his hair, lovingly placing it in a diary in which he thought she ought to start writing. She read the words on the first page; she didn't even recognise his handwriting.

'To my Beloved! I am with you. Everything will be fine. A book to fill with memories of all the wonderful things that await us.'

Astonished, she read the lines again. Who was he, really? What other secret sides did he have that she hadn't managed to discover or coax out during all their years together? All she knew was that what she held in her hand was an honest attempt on his part to show that he loved her. That he was ready to do whatever it took. Perhaps this was what he had realised over the past few days. That he really wanted to try again.

She suddenly felt tears welling up, and the rage and hatred that had been driving her forward in recent days yielded to a tremendous sorrow. The weariness that came over her when she relaxed a little was overwhelming. She crawled under the bedspread, exhausted. Maybe there was another possibility? But how could she ever forgive him? Ever trust him again? But what kind of mother would she be if she didn't give him a real chance, for Axel's sake? It wasn't the fact that he had fallen in love with another woman that was unforgivable; considering the state of their marriage, it was even understandable. It was the wound from his betrayal and his lies that would never heal. The insulting fact that he never told her, explained, gave her a chance to react and take a stand. The fact that the person she thought stood closest to her could do her so wrong, all for his own benefit. How could she ever feel respect for him again?

She lay back on the pillow and closed her eyes. Just to be able to sleep, close her eyes to it all, and then wake up from this nightmare with everything back to normal.

Perhaps only a few words from him would be sufficient. A few words, uttered sincerely and in complete honesty, perhaps that was all she needed to give him another chance. To be able to respect him as a man.

A sincere and honest: I'm sorry. Please forgive me.

She woke up when the bedroom door was thrown open. With a bang the handle made a deep dent in the soft plaster wall, and the sound made her sit up in sheer terror. He was standing on the threshold, and the expression on his face scared her.

'God, what a fucking pig you are!'

She glanced at the clock radio. Quarter past five. She had slept for over six hours.

'What is it?'

Careful now.

He snorted.

'What is it? Well, what the hell do you think it is? It never occurred to you that I ought to be the first to find out we're getting a divorce and that you intend to throw me out of the house?'

She stopped breathing.

'How the fuck do you think it feels to find out from your parents? Standing there like a fucking idiot, not understanding a thing.'

Her heart was pounding. Drop by drop the control was seeping out of her.

'Why were you talking to them?'

Her question was idiotic, she could hear that herself. He thought so, too, and shook his head in utter disgust.

'Because they wondered when we were going to pick up Axel.'

Shit. Everything was going to pieces.

'What would it be like if you decided to cut off that umbilical cord one day? Living with you is like being fucking married to your parents too. They're like a . . . like a fucking sticky slime that covers everything. Oh, they were *so* understanding!'

He mimicked her mother's voice and said:

'*Poor little Henrik, how ARE you?*'

His whole body showed the repugnance he felt.

'How the hell can you go to them and blab about everything before you talk to me? But it's obvious, because that's what you've always done. Why should a little divorce make any difference? It's their damned fault it turned out like this.'

Her fury was instant.

'My parents have always been willing to help us out. That's a hell of a lot more than I can say about yours!'

'At least they leave us in peace.'

'You can say that again!'

'It's better than the way yours carry on. You've always put your parents ahead of me. As if they were the ones who were your real family.'

'Well, they are.'

'There, you see! Why don't you go and have a kid with them, too, then? And move in with them. Then you can keep on fucking your lover as usual.'

He slammed his fist into the door jamb and rushed out to the kitchen. She followed him. He was leaning over the counter and breathing hard, his chest heaving with the effort.

How could he have the nerve?

'What the hell do you mean by that?'

He turned his head and looked at her.

'You can stop playing games now. He told me all about it.'

'What fucking 'he' are you talking about?'

A condescending smile slid across his face.

'How can you be so pathetic? There's a lot I could say about you, but I had no idea you were such a coward.'

'You're calling *me* a coward?'

He didn't reply. She realised that her remark had hit home and that she had the upper hand again. But for how long? What was she allowed to know and not know? She wasn't allowed to know about Linda, who at the same time was her only defence for what she had done. But now her well-devised scheme had been shattered and ended up in disarray. Everything could be turned against her.

'Who is this "he" and what did he say?'

'Come off it, Eva. I'm telling you that I already know what you're up to, so you can stop playing games. Did you think he was going to move in here after you threw me out?'

'Who is this fucking 'he' you're talking about?'

With a sweep of his arm he knocked the fruit bowl to the floor. Apples and oranges rolled across the polished hardwood floor, scattering around the sharp ceramic shards.

He headed for the bedroom.

She followed.

'Why don't you answer instead of diverting your rage to something else? It wasn't the fruit bowl's fault that you don't have an answer.'

He pulled out the top drawer of the bureau and started rummaging round in her underwear.

'What are you doing?'

'Where is it?'

'What?'

'That fine new diary that you've got.'

'Do you want to take it back or what?'

He stopped and stared at her.

'All right, that's enough! I put it out on the bed for you. I've already seen it and that disgusting lock of hair. How old is he, anyway? Did you exchange lockets too? How sweet if you went around with a little golden lock of hair round your neck from now on.'

He held up the black lace bra and waved it in front of her face.

'I presume he gets turned on when you wear this, although I can't see why.'

She stood mute. Had he completely lost his mind?

He slammed the drawer shut and left the room. She caught up with him in the doorway to the living room, where he suddenly stopped.

'You're really sick in the head.'

He sounded like he really meant what he said, and she followed his gaze. On the coffee table stood the vase with the green stalks in it. The roses themselves had vanished without a trace. Cut off and removed.

Now it was her turn to snort.

'That's really going too far. You could have saved yourself the trouble, I didn't want them anyway.'

He turned his head and looked at her with an expression as if she were utterly mad.

The phone rang. Neither of them made a move to

answer it. It rang and rang, and they stood like statues, ignoring the phone.

'Let it ring.'

He turned at once and went to the phone in the kitchen. As if her words were a direct order to pick it up.

'Yes, this is Henrik.'

Then there was silence. It went on so long that she walked over to look in the doorway. He was standing completely still with his mouth open, staring into space with the receiver pressed to his ear.

'How is she doing then? Which hospital is she in?'

Suddenly nervous. His mother had had a bypass operation a few months ago. Maybe she had a relapse.

Then he turned his head slowly and looked at her. Fixed his eyes on her with a look so full of loathing and hostility that it scared her. Without looking away he kept talking.

'You can tell her yourself.'

He held out the phone to her.

'Who is it?'

He didn't answer. Just continued hating her and held out the phone.

She went slowly over to him; there was a palpable sense of danger. He kept staring at her when she put the receiver to her ear.

'Hello?'

'This is Kerstin Evertsson from Kortbacken pre-school.'

Formal and impersonal. Someone she didn't know. Or someone who preferred not to know her.

'Yes, hi.'

'I might as well get straight to the point. I've just

told your husband that I know he and Linda Persson had a relationship which was terminated yesterday. I also told him that Åsa Sandström received an anonymous letter with a newspaper article about Linda and that you were the one who put it in her mailbox. Åsa saw you when you did it.'

Good God, let me disappear. Let me not have to go through this.

'Naturally I was obliged to call Linda and tell her this, even though I already knew all about the trial and everything else she had been through. But for Linda it was more than she could bear. She's in intensive care at the Söder Hospital after slashing her wrists.'

She briefly met Henrik's black look before she glanced away.

'I also think you should know that the parents' group has collected money for flowers and that they will be asking Linda to continue working here if she pulls through.'

She would never be able to show herself in public again.

'I have to confess that I don't really know how we should resolve the rest. For Axel's sake, of course, it's obvious that he should keep his place here, but I have to say it feels extremely difficult to keep you as clients. I'll leave the decision up to you.'

Help me. Good God, help me.

'Are you still there?'

'Yes.'

'Then it would be good if you got hold of Åsa Sandström, because she wants to talk with you. She wants an explanation for why you involved her in all this. Because now everyone understands who sent all those emails too, which you claimed were from Linda. Surely you must see that Åsa feels used and rightly so. She's upset about this, to say the least.'

She couldn't breathe.

This was intolerable.

'As you can hear, I'm furious about what you've done, and I'd be lying if I said anything else. I can understand that it must have felt, well, I don't know, bloody awful, when you realised that Henrik and Linda were having an affair, but that does not excuse what you've done. Here we work day after day to teach the children about right and wrong, and that one must always take responsibility for one's actions. I thought I knew you, but obviously I don't.'

Shame was a snare, growing tighter with each syllable. She was annihilated, deprived of all honour. She had to get away. Away from Nacka. Away from Sweden. Away from any chance of meeting anyone who might recognise her and know what she had done.

'Is she going to be all right?'

'They don't know yet.'

She put down the receiver, forgetting to hang up. Henrik with his arms crossed. Hateful, hostile, and forever with right on his side.

Down the stairs.

Shoes. She remembered that you had to have shoes on when you went outside.

Not Värmdövägen. She had to stay on the side streets.

The houses surrounding her, the lamps lit in their windows, families just coming home, reunited after another work day. All of it just a decoration to punish her. Not for sale. Inaccessible. Henceforth you shall only look, never take part. You are banished from our community. Outlawed for all time, but remembered.

As if through a dirty filter she saw a car approaching, and she reached back to pull up her hood. Not be seen. The hood wasn't where it was supposed to be. She looked down and noticed that her jacket too was missing. The car passed by. She had to go further, had to get away.

At first she didn't notice the car creeping along next to her. Only noticed something white out of the corner of her eye. Then it drove past her and stopped. Someone got out.

'Hi.'

A surprised voice that sounded glad.

Nobody could be glad to see her.

She stopped. Something familiar about the figure whose face was dimly lit by a street light.

'Imagine meeting you here, do you live around here?'

Colourful pictures. The voice associated with abstract patterns.

'How are you doing, anyway? Can I drive you somewhere?'

Everything empty. And then this person, sounding so worried for her sake, who still lowered himself to talk to her. Then she saw Daniel's parents walking towards her farther down the street. Each carrying a briefcase. On their way home from the bus. Soon they would see her. Flowers for Linda. They knew what she had done and had contributed money for flowers for Linda today. No side street to escape into.

She went over to the passenger side and climbed in.

Just take me away from here.

Let me get out of meeting Daniel's parents.

What could possibly be worse?

If only she hadn't.

So many 'if only she hadn't's. So many that it was no longer possible to see when the first one occurred.

They sat in complete silence. He didn't ask where she wanted to go and she didn't wonder where he was headed. Just leaned her head back against the head-rest and closed her eyes. A silent zone where she was not subject to accusations.

She didn't open her eyes until the car stopped and the engine was turned off. A cul-de-sac. Some parked cars. Blocks of flats. She remembered the last time she was here.

With an effort of will she turned her head and looked at him. Took in his warm smile and lowered her eyes, let her gaze settle on his hands resting on the steering wheel. She remembered their clumsiness, his fumbling fingers running over her body; she was amazed that he had even dared.

Again an 'if only she hadn't'.

'Thanks for the lift.'

She made a move to open the door. The exhaustion felt like an ache in her joints, a physical plea not to have to move.

'Wouldn't you like to come in for a while?'

She let her hand rest on the door handle as she

searched for an answer. There was anticipation in his voice, and that was more than she could bear. She opened the car door and the cold that struck her reminded her that she had no jacket. Or money.

She had nothing.

'I have some pear cider at my place. Won't you come in and have a glass? To be honest, you look like you could use it. Then I can drive you wherever you like later.'

Wherever you like. Where was that? Was there such a place?

If only she hadn't.

The whole past chain of events was linked by the 'if only she hadn't's.

But the first link in the chain was Henrik's. The betrayal. His cowardice. The rage he had directed at her. His lack of consideration.

Kerstin's judgement echoed in her mind. One must always take responsibility for one's actions. What did Kerstin know about how Henrik had acted towards her? What he had done to provoke her crime. The impotence she felt. But she would never get the chance to defend herself. Not before any of those who thought they had the right to judge her. The verdict had been handed down and the sentence passed.

Pariah.

But what about Henrik? Didn't any part of the blame fall on him? Because he was the one who had prompted the whole chain of 'what if she hadn't's.

He got out of the car and she saw through the windscreen that he was walking towards her open door. When he got there he held out his hand to her.

'Come on now. Just a glass of pear cider. That's all.'

So tired, through and through. All the way into her marrow. If only she could just follow along, not have to make any decisions.

'Just a glass of pear cider?'

He smiled and nodded.

'Just a glass of pear cider.'

She refused his outstretched hand and got out of the car, moving past him. He let his arm hover in the air a bit too long before he slowly let it drop, closed her door and fetched a plastic bag from the boot.

'Come on.'

He started towards the door of his building. Maybe she was angry when she refused his hand; she didn't mean to seem unpleasant, she just didn't want to give him any ideas, not a single hope of anything more than what they had agreed. A glass of pear cider. Nothing more. That's what he had said and she had accepted.

He turned on the light in the stairwell and showed her in with a gentlemanly gesture, inviting her to go first. He followed a few steps behind. She was filled by a slight uneasiness at his presence, well aware that he had her rear end in his view. She felt exposed and open to his eyes, which could look at whatever they liked. She leaned her back against the wall as he unlocked the door. Four locks.

The last time. The nervousness she felt and how she had pressed herself against him to conceal it. How the images of Henrik and Linda had made her conquer her distaste.

Five days ago.

She stopped inside the door, heard him stick a key in one of the locks and turn it. And then the rattle of the keyring to lock the others and the rustle of the plastic bag he had taken out of the boot.

And she suddenly recalled that he thought her name was Linda. That her camouflage back then had made her brave enough to fulfil her intentions.

If only she hadn't.

Yet another one.

But now there was no reason why she should reveal her real name. It would just provoke questions that she didn't want to answer.

'Welcome. Welcome back, I should say.'

She wasn't back. The woman who stood before him was here for the first time.

She looked down at her shoes as if it were an impossible task to bend down and take them off. He followed her gaze, knelt down and carefully pulled down the zippers on the inside of her ankles. He placed her hand on his shoulder so she could lean on him as he pulled off her shoes. He held her right foot in his hand for a moment too long, and she could suddenly hear his breathing. She couldn't put up any resistance, just stood there with her hand on his shoulder and let him hold her right foot. She shouldn't be here. She ought to leave. But where could she go? And how could she find the energy?

He stood up, gently touched her elbow, led her into the little kitchen and sat her down on one of the chairs. She watched him take two steps over to the refrigerator and caught a glimpse of its contents when he opened it. All three shelves filled with recumbent cider bottles. He took out two, pulled his key chain out of his pocket, and opened them with a red bottle opener squeezed in between the keys. Then he stood with the bottles in his hands, cocked his head to one side and looked at her.

'How are you doing, anyway?'

She couldn't say a word.

'I don't have a sofa, but you can sit on the bed in there instead. I mean if you want to be a bit more comfortable, that's all. You look like you need a rest. I can sit on the floor.'

'I'm fine here.'

He sat down on the chair on the other side of the fold-down table, leaned forward and handed her one of the bottles of cider.

'Cheers. Once again.'

He smiled and she raised the bottle and drank.

'That's the kind you like, isn't it?'

She read the label on the bottle. Couldn't tell if this one tasted either better or worse than those she had tasted before.

'Sure.'

'Imagine running into each other again like this. It's really too wild to be just a coincidence, it almost feels like it means something, as if it was fate.'

She couldn't come up with any good answer but smiled a little so she wouldn't seem rude.

For a while they sat in silence. Then he got up and went over to the small kitchen counter, picked up the dishrag and wiped off the stainless steel surface. He rubbed it intently and kept checking to see whether the spot was gone.

'Can you tell me what happened?'

He rinsed out the dishrag and wrung it out, rinsed

it again and repeated the procedure one more time before he folded it in thirds and hung it over the tap.

'Why you're out walking without a jacket, for example, and where you were going?'

He straightened the dishrag and moved it a few centimetres out on the tap.

She took a gulp from the bottle.

'If you don't mind, I just can't talk about it.'

She had no obligations to him. No duty to share anything with him. On the contrary. If she told him, the free zone she had found would be eradicated, he would join the jury and judge her.

Linda in intensive care. If she pulls through we're going to ask her to keep working here.

If she pulls through.

She took another drink, looking for respite in intoxication.

He stood completely still with his back to her. Then he suddenly turned around.

'You can take a bath if you like.'

She didn't answer, but felt her suspicions awaken at once.

He put down the bottle on the table.

'You don't have to be afraid. I'll run the bath for you and sit out here and relax. I think it would be nice for you to take a bath; you of all people certainly deserve to rest a little.'

Then he was gone, and she heard the sound of running water.

She had no intention of taking off her clothes in the flat, but in the bathroom she could lock herself in and then she wouldn't have to answer any questions. Wouldn't have to talk at all. And she'd have a chance to think. Maybe she could ring Sara or Gerd at work and ask if she could stay overnight, figure out some plausible explanation.

His voice from the bathroom and then suddenly the familiar aroma.

'I've bought new bubble bath too. Eucalyptus.'

The same that she had in her bathroom at home. Which was a present from Axel. She took it as a sign, gave up struggling and allowed herself to relax.

He had good intentions.

And that's what she needed right now.

She took the last gulp from the bottle and heard the water turned off in the bathtub. Then he appeared in the doorway.

'Your bath is ready.'

He smiled and gestured towards the bathroom, but noticed that her bottle was empty. At once he was at the refrigerator to fetch a new one. She stood up, and he made a move to touch her forearm to lead her once again, but he caught himself and withdrew. Perhaps out of consideration, perhaps he wanted to show that she was safe, that he had no ulterior motives.

She took the new bottle and went into the hall towards the open bathroom door. The bathtub was filled to the brim and the white bubbles were crackling invitingly. Her mood was improving. She could use a little rest.

'Here's a towel for you.'

He handed her a light-blue bath towel. Carefully folded, edge to edge, to the last centimetre. She took it and put it on the toilet seat. The towel reluctantly unfolded but the creases left deep traces in the terrycloth. She turned to him. He was standing in the doorway. She made no move to start undressing, and he clearly understood her unspoken demand.

'Enjoy yourself now, and don't hurry. Take all the time you want.'

'Thank you.'

He backed out and pulled the door shut; she turned the lock until the white half-moon turned to red. Then she slowly took off her clothes and sank down through the foam with the bottle on the edge of the tub. A calm began to spread over her. The cider had done its job.

It was Nacka that was the problem. She had to get away. She could already sense how she felt free having left the boundaries of the town. Here she could breathe again. She could think clearly enough to realise that even if she had done wrong, the guilt was not hers alone. There was a reason for her actions. What if they sold the house and she moved into the city, let Axel start at a new pre-school where no one knew them?

She took another gulp.

Things would work out. There was still a future.

'Is the bath nice?'

His voice just outside the door.

'Yes, it is. Thanks.'

Just when she thought he had left, he said something else. He sounded even closer now, as if his mouth were right next to the crack in the door.

'I don't mean you any harm, on the contrary. You know that, don't you?'

A pang of uneasiness in the midst of the soothing bath foam.

'Yes.'

'Good.'

She had just settled back again and closed her eyes when she heard the sound. She turned her head and saw the red half-moon turn until it was white, and the next moment he was standing in the open doorway. She sank down as deep as she could to cover herself with the bubbles.

'I would like to be left in peace in here, please.'

He smiled at her.

'You are at peace in here.'

He picked up the bath towel and placed it on his lap as he sat down on the toilet seat.

'I mean alone.'

He smiled again, sadly this time, as if she didn't know what was good for her.

'Haven't you been alone long enough?'

She suddenly felt afraid. Wanted to get up and leave the flat. But not as long as he could see her.

'Why do you look so scared? I already know how beautiful you are. You've already showed me once, and how could I ever forget?'

'I said that we were just going to drink a pear cider.'

'That's right. And now we've drunk two of them. And you can have just as many as you like. I bought them for you.'

There was nothing threatening about him, he radiated nothing but genuine goodwill. And yet there was something that told her she ought to get out of here, get away as fast as she could.

'Wait a minute and I'll give you something beautiful to wear after you're done with your bath.'

He stood up.

'That's not necessary, I'll wear my own clothes.'

'You're worth something more beautiful than those.'

He snatched up her clothes and took the bath towel with him as he vanished into the hall. As quickly as she could, she got up and grabbed the guest hand towel. She had to get out of here. The bath foam slid around on her skin as if the hand towel were waterproof.

Then he was back in the doorway.

She tried to hide herself as best she could.

He stopped in mid-stride and stood there quite still. As if he had forgotten she was in there and now he saw her for the first time. Embarrassed, he lowered his eyes when he saw her nakedness.

'Excuse me.'

'Give me the towel.'

With infinite slowness his gaze moved closer and closer. Along the floor and across the bath mat, then up the bathtub, across tile after tile his eyes made their way towards her. When they reached her naked body which she was so desperately trying to hide behind the tiny towel, she saw undisguised admiration in his face. A gasp when his eyes reached her thighs and slowly swept across the towel to meet the skin again above her breasts.

'God, how beautiful you are.'

His voice was shaking.

'Give me the towel!'

Her sharp words jolted his gaze away and he again stared down at the floor. Then he put something down on the toilet seat, backed out and closed the door behind him.

She quickly got out of the tub and tried to dry herself as best she could.

'Give me my clothes!'

'It's on the toilet seat.'

She jumped at the closeness of his voice, his mouth sounded like it was pressed against the door outside.

She snatched whatever it was he had put on the seat. Never in her life. Lined and made of a glossy fabric with tufts in the most worn places.

An old flowery dressing gown.

'I want my clothes!'

'Do you have to sound so angry? They're soaking in the sink. Put on the dressing gown now and come out, then we'll talk about all this.'

His voice was still very close to her.

There was something wrong with him, she had no doubt about that. But how dangerous was he, how scared did she need to be? All she knew with certainty was that she wanted to get out of here, and now she had no clothes. And no one in the entire world would be looking for her. And even if someone actually was trying to find her, nobody knew where she was. She had to leave the bathroom. Go out and talk to him. But to 'talk about all this' seemed like a contradiction. They had absolutely nothing to do with each other, and that's precisely what she had to make him realise.

Disgusted, she looked at the dressing gown. There was a brown ring of dirt around the inside of the collar. Then she managed to get the better of her repugnance and put it on, trying to ignore the odour of age-old filth and a musty wardrobe.

She put her hand on the door handle and took a deep breath.

'I'm coming out now.'

Not a sound was heard from outside.

She cautiously opened the door a crack. It was dark out there, the hall light was turned off. Out of pure impulse she turned off the bathroom light so she could disappear in the darkness. She opened the door a bit more and when she looked out she saw the glow of a candle from the room. She cast a glance at the front door, well aware that she had heard the keys being turned in all four of the locks. Keys that now lay in the pocket of his trousers.

She took a step towards the candlelight. Everything was quiet. Then she stopped. One more step and she would be visible to him through the doorway. The sudden sound of his voice made her jump.

'Come.'

She didn't move from the spot.

'Please, come. I didn't mean to frighten you.'

'What is it you want? Why can't I have my clothes?'

'Of course you'll get your clothes, but they're wet right now. Come in here and we can talk a bit while they dry.'

What choice did she have? She took the last step and looked into the room. He was sitting on the edge of the bed. From her feet in the doorway where she stood and over to his feet by the bed, an avenue of votive candles. A planned path along the floor which all too obviously visualised his expectations. She was just about to protest and explain that no matter what had happened the last time she was there, it was never going to happen again. But then she saw his face and stopped short. It wasn't her he was looking at, not her eyes he sought. He was looking at the flowered dressing gown. And suddenly, utterly without warning, his face was distorted in a grimace and his whole body shrank, collapsed. He looked away and she saw that he was trying to hide the fact that he was crying. Her confusion was absolute. What was it he actually wanted?

She didn't say a word. Just stood there in the doorway watching him, and his whole bearing revealed a failed attempt to defend himself from her unwelcome stare. He sobbed a couple of times and sat looking down at the floor, rubbing his hand over his face. Then he hesitantly glanced at her again, timid and embarrassed.

'Forgive me.'

She didn't reply. She realised in the midst of it all that the room had changed. The walls were bare but with black dots from the nail holes where the strange paintings had hung.

He looked down at the floor and the votive candles again.

'I haven't dared to light candles for several years, but then I bought some in case you were here.'

He uttered the words like an awkward confession, as naked before her as she had been before him in the bathroom. As if he wanted to reveal himself in return, as an excuse for his intrusion. Her fear dropped away. He had merely read the wrong signals when she came home with him. And could she actually blame him? He had naturally believed that she would call. That their night together was a prelude. Seen her as a possibility.

What if she stayed for a little while and made him realise that she wasn't, that what had happened was a mistake and that she hadn't meant to hurt him? He wasn't dangerous, he had only fallen in love and forgotten to find out if she felt the same way.

'Why haven't you lit candles for years?'

An attempt at conversation. Approach cautiously and gradually get him to understand.

He looked at her and smiled slightly.

'There is so much you don't know about me, that I haven't managed to tell you yet.'

Wrong track. She had to try and be crystal clear from the beginning.

He beat her to it before she could start over.

'I would like to ask you a favour.'

'What kind of favour?'

He swallowed.

'I would like you to come and sit next to me while you have that on.'

She looked down at the disgusting dressing gown.

'Why is that?'

He hesitated a long time before continuing, she could see that the words came from deep inside him, that he had to muster his courage to speak his request.

'I just want you to let me put my head in your lap for a while.'

Almost inaudible. Embarrassed and with his eyes looking down at his hands in his lap.

It was impossible to be afraid of anyone so pitiful. She might as well tell him the truth right away so she could get out of there.

'I can understand that you may have thought that I, or that we, when we . . . Well, it wasn't that it was bad or anything like that, but what happened was a mistake, I was drunk and not thinking. Maybe you hoped we would see each other again, but it's better that I just tell you the truth. I'm married.'

He sat expressionless. His lack of reaction encouraged her to continue. Why hadn't she told him the truth from the start? She of all people should know that honesty worked best.

'Maybe I could borrow some clothes from you and then I'll send them back later. My husband will worry if I don't come home soon.'

'Why should he?'

His voice was suddenly hard and cold. All goodwill gone.

'Of course he'll be worried if I don't come home.'

She could hear the new tone in her own voice. More cautious now.

He shrugged his shoulders.

'That depends, of course, on what type of marriage you have. Whether you love each other or not. Or if you make a habit of being unfaithful.'

Hurt. Proud and hurt. A dangerous combination. She had to proceed more carefully, his temporary vulnerability had thrown her off the track.

'I don't make a habit of being unfaithful. With you was the first time.'

He snorted.

'What an honour.'

Shit. Wrong again. She had to choose her words better. He was like a minefield.

'I didn't mean to hurt you in any way. I mean, we're two grown people. We were kind to each other for a while.'

'You mean I was kind to you for a while, don't you? You used me as consolation when your husband at home wasn't doing his part any more, right? Or was it to make him jealous, or did you want revenge for something?'

She stood silent.

'Where in the midst of everything did you think that I would wind up, after you had used me?'

She didn't reply. Couldn't think of any other reason than that every single person takes responsibility for his own life, but right now she didn't think she had the right to say those words. Everything had broken down. She had to get out of there.

'I told you I made a mistake. What more can I say than I'm sorry?'

'And your husband? Do you love him?'

No.

'Yes.'

'And if he were unfaithful to you? What would you do then?'

She swallowed.

'I'm not sure. I would probably try to forgive him. Everybody makes mistakes.'

His eyes narrowed.

'Nobody who betrays someone deserves to be forgiven. A betrayal can never be forgiven, will never be forgotten, it stays inside like an open wound. Something is torn apart and can never again be made whole.'

She wasn't the only one in the room who knew how it felt, that was quite obvious. But she had no desire to share her own experiences with him.

He went on.

'If there was a man who loved you above all else, who was ready to do anything for you, who would solemnly promise that he would never betray you, that he would always be there for you, standing by your side, would you love him in return?'

She swallowed again and looked down at the floor, fixing her eyes on one of the candles.

'That's not exactly how love works, is it?'

'Then how does it work?'

'It goes wherever it wants. It's not something you can control. If you fall in love, then you fall in love.'

'Is it that simple? Can't a person do anything to make love grow or make it last?'

She didn't answer. She couldn't.

'You don't think so?'

'I don't know. I'm no expert.'

'But what exactly is a betrayal? And why does it hurt so much if you know that the person betraying you can't even help it? That love has just gone where it wants.'

Her weary brain made a brave attempt to follow his logic. 'The betrayal is the fact that someone lies. That the one you trust is lying right to your face.'

'So if he goes to bed with someone else and admits it, then it's OK?'

'Of course not.'

'But it should be OK. He can't decide for himself if he wants to fall in love or not, you said that yourself. So if he confesses then everything would have to be all right, wouldn't it?'

She sighed.

'It's one thing to fall in love, but quite another what you do about it.'

'So the fact that he loves someone else is not a betrayal?'

She was starting to get really irritated by his questions. Get a life, then you'll see how easy it is.

'I don't know. Can I borrow some clothes now?'

'So you think that if someone stops loving the one he ought to love, then it's best not to say anything? Just keep going as usual and pretend everything is the way it should be?'

She didn't answer.

'Isn't that a kind of betrayal too? That the one you think loves you is really just staying with you out of duty and consideration?'

She looked down at the floor again.

He went on. 'What about all the people who actually live their whole lives together and are happy? If it's like you say it is, they were just lucky. It didn't have anything to do with how they actually behaved?'

When she didn't answer he stood up and went over to the window. Stood there with his back to her. Then he gave a heavy sigh and went back and sat down.

'So you don't think it's possible to learn to love another person, decide to love him and then do one's best?'

'No. I don't believe that.'

Now he had got his answer. Now she wanted to leave.

He sat with his head bowed and his hands in his lap. So naïve. He thought that he loved her, he didn't even know her, didn't even know her name.

'Please, can I borrow some clothes now?'

Slowly he looked up at her again. The disappointment in his face was obvious.

'Are you in such a hurry to leave?'

In silence their eyes met. She gave up, turned and

went out to the kitchen; he hadn't been lying, he had really put her clothes to soak in the sink.

Fucking idiot.

She met him in the hall on her way back. In his outstretched hands he held a pair of folded jeans and a red college pullover. She took them gratefully.

'Thanks. I'll send them back later.'

He made no comment. Merely nodded towards the bathroom.

'You can change in there.'

'Thanks.'

'Just one thing.'

Her only thought was to leave.

'I'd be happy to give you a lift somewhere if you like, but there's something I'd really like to show you before we leave. Maybe you might consider doing this for me, as a sort of farewell. It will only take a couple of minutes.'

Anything, as long as he unlocked the door afterwards.

'Of course. What is it?'

'It's outside.'

Even better.

She went into the bathroom and changed. She heard him rattling his keys in the front door and hurried as best she could. He had a jacket and shoes on when she came out, and she quickly bent down and pulled hers on. He stood quietly inside the front door with the plastic bag he had taken from the boot of the car in his hand.

'Are you ready?'

She nodded.

'And you promise I can show you this?'

She nodded again.

'Cross your heart?'

'Yes.'

Let me out now, for God's sake!

He went out in the stairwell and turned on the light. He pushed in the light button four times although the lights went on after the first one, and then locked the top lock. Then back to the light button to press it again before he locked the second one. She watched in astonishment the strange procedure and at the same time took the opportunity to wonder where he was taking her. Everything would have been much easier if she at least had her wallet.

They went down the stairs in silence. She first, he following. On the ground floor he passed her and she saw how he pulled down the sleeve of his jumper as protection before he touched the handle of the front door.

Then they were outside.

'It's down here, just below the common.'

She hesitated. A path leading into the woods.

'You promised.'

Something in his tone made her realise that she had better keep her promise.

'What is it?'

'You'll see. But it's something really beautiful.'

They started walking. The path sloped down and soon she glimpsed water between the trees. He didn't say a word. Just below the common, he had said, but their walk was a good bit longer. She was just about to protest, plead that it was too cold, but didn't.

'Here. It's over here.'

A house and a sign but it was too dark to see what

it said. An iron gate and a chain-link fence around it. He turned off the walking path, went over to the fence and raised it so there was about half a metre's room between the ground and the bottom of the fence. He nodded to her to crawl under it.

'Can we really go in here?'

'There's no danger, I've been here plenty of times. Don't worry about getting dirt on those jeans.'

She didn't want to, but she had promised. If she refused now, she'd have to walk back to town. She sighed, got down on all fours and crawled under the fence, stood up and brushed off her knees.

He followed.

She looked around. Boats covered by tarpaulins. 'No trespassing.' The sign was readable now: 'Årstadals Boat Club'.

'Where are we going?'

'Just out on the wharf over there. The one on the right.'

It was cold without a jacket and she shivered as they made their way through the boats to reach the wharf. Then they went out on the pier and she did as he said, followed it to the right. He was right behind her. When she reached the end of the pier she stopped and looked around. The woods to her right, to her left the island of Södermalm across the water.

She turned around.

'What was it you wanted to show me?'

He gazed out across the black water, as if he wanted to draw out his answer as long as possible.

'Something you have never seen or experienced before.'

'And what's that?'

She felt impatient now. Impatient and freezing.

He stood completely still. Then he placed his hand over his heart.

'Here.'

'Come on now, stop it. I want to go now. If you don't intend to give me a lift then I'll walk.'

A furrow between his eyebrows.

'Why are you always in such a hurry?'

'I'm freezing.'

She regretted the words at once, they could be taken as an invitation to warm her up.

He looked out over the water again.

'I'm going to show you what real love is.'

And then his eyes back to hers.

'If you have time for it.'

This was starting to feel unpleasant, but her irritation was greater than her fear.

'But I've already explained that I'm married. I thought we were finished talking about that.'

'You understand that real love is when you love someone so much that you're prepared to do anything to get the one you love.'

'Oh please . . .'

He interrupted her.

'That's how much I love you.'

'You don't even know me. You have no idea who I am. And whatever you say, you can't force me to love you, it doesn't work that way. I love my husband.'

Suddenly he looked sad.

'All I want is for you to be happy. Why can't you let me make you happy?'

'I really have to go now.'

He took a step to the side and blocked her way.

She tried to pass him on the other side but he blocked her again.

Her uneasiness was growing stronger and she realised that it was best to admit it.

'You're scaring me.'

He smiled sadly and shook his head.

'How can you be afraid of me? I've told you that I love you. He, on the other hand, the one you're in such a hurry to go home to . . . Why don't you just let him go? Or even better, tell him to go to hell.'

She rubbed her arms to try and warm up.

'Because I love him, that's why.'

He sighed.

'How can someone like you love a man like that? You deserve someone so much better. And Eva, if you want to be completely honest with yourself, deep inside you know that he doesn't love you any more.'

A sudden jolt through her body.

Eva? What the hell. Eva?

'How . . .'

She couldn't find words to formulate the question. Everything had suddenly changed.

'It's so sad to see a woman like you believe that you have to be like Linda to be loved. That you even use her name. Linda is a whore, she's nothing compared to you.'

She stood mute. Mute and suddenly robbed of all frame of reference. Who was this man in front of her? How could he know? She was scared now, really scared, robbed of all control. Every cell in her body signalled that she had to defend herself. That he was a greater threat than she could ever have imagined.

'How could you be so stupid to believe that some

roses had made him change. I know how jerks like that operate.'

He lifted the plastic bag he had brought with him and emptied it over her head. Instinctively she put her hands up in front of her face to shield herself. She felt the contents fall over her and all around her. And then the smell. She looked down at her feet. Twenty red roses. Cut off and stolen from her coffee table.

She stared at him, terror-stricken.

'Now, on the other hand, now you are receiving them out of true love. But I, I who truly love you, love you for who you are, I'm not even allowed to rest my head for a while on your lap.'

She looked around. Water on all sides. Not a person to be seen. A train passed by on the bridge far off behind him. The sounds of the city. All quite close but out of reach.

'I wanted to give you time to understand that you can trust me. That I will always be there for you. I've already got to know Axel, so it wouldn't have been any problem if we just took it easy in the beginning. But you don't want to. You're forcing me to prove how much I love you.'

She backed up a step, felt with her foot behind her and realised that she was dangerously close to the edge. Then he took a step towards her, put his hands on her shoulders and looked straight into her eyes.

'I love you.'

She never felt the fall. Only an icy cold surrounding her and pressing all the air out of her lungs. Her body came up to the surface and took a deep gasping breath, with a furious will to survive. She reached out for the pier but couldn't find it. In the next moment something closed around her body and pulled her down, down below the surface. With all her strength she struggled to keep her head above water, arms flailing as she tried to defend herself against the weight. Then she suddenly felt his lips on hers, his tongue pressing into her mouth. His legs clamped her in an iron grip and pressed her down, down into the darkness, down in the icy cold. Time did not exist. Only the terror of everything unfinished, that it was all too late now. Then she felt her resistance start to fade, how she slowly but surely yielded to his will and gave in.

Silence. And in the silence she heard more than she had ever heard before.

A boundless silence. Behind her, in front of her, all around.

She willingly surrendered herself to the peace that surrounded her.

Finally.

She didn't have to fight any longer.

Everything was good.

'Maybe you think I'm foolish, sitting here talking to you like this, but somewhere I'm sure you can hear me. I don't know if you can understand, but it feels so clear that you will always be a part of me, maybe that's how it is for all mothers, that the bond is never really cut, it just becomes extra clear when . . . oh Eva . . . my beloved, lovely little Eva, how could it turn out like this?

'Forgive me. It doesn't do any of us any good for me to sit here and cry but . . . it's just so empty and lonely without you. Your father, he, I don't know, we try to support each other as best we can but he, he can't even bear to come here, even though I tell him it would surely be good for him.

'Oh, if you could only give me a sign, anything at all, just show me somehow that you can hear me.

'Axel asks about you all the time, it's hard to know what's the right thing to say. He's started going to a different day-care as well, but I don't quite under-stand why it was necessary to do that, now that . . . but Henrik refused to listen. He got so angry when I tried to convince him to let Axel stay where he was. I only thought it would have been best for him if everything didn't have to change all at once. And you two, who did so much socialising with the other day-care parents. And in the neighbourhood. You used to have such a good time. We saw the boy that Axel used to play with, the dark-haired one. Is his name David or Daniel, I don't remember? Anyway, he and his parents walked past on the street while we were out in the garden. Yes, Erik was there too, because we were helping Henrik saw down some bushes but Axel was in the house. Anyway, I thought it was a bit strange because they just walked right by as if they didn't see us, or rather as if they didn't want to see us. And Henrik, he just stood there and didn't try to make contact either. I don't know, I thought it felt odd, the two of you used to see them a lot, I thought. But maybe it's hard for them to know what to say to us now that . . . People behave so strangely. I would like nothing better than for people to talk about you.

'Little Axel. He's grown so quiet. I've tried to get him to talk about how he feels, but . . . he doesn't say much, he's just waiting for you to come home. But things are going better and better at the new day-care, even though he wants me to stay with him there. Yes, I'm the one who has to take him there because Henrik, he . . . well, I don't know but I should probably tell you the truth, we're quite worried about him, I think he's actually started drinking too much. Several times when I've called in the middle of the day it sounded like he was quite drunk, actually. It feels as though he's isolating himself more and more, he doesn't even seem to be working just now.

'It's so hard to know what to do, it's obvious that

we're worried about how Axel is doing. How he'll react to all this in the long run. We've told Henrik that Axel can stay with us as often as he likes, or that we can come there if it feels more comfortable to be at home, but . . . I think he wants to sell the house and move out. We're trying to talk him into waiting a little longer, until we know for sure that . . . I know how much you'd like to stay living there.

'Oh, it makes me so mad when I think about all you had ahead of you, once you'd finally made up your mind to make a change.

'I'd so like to be able to ask you if it's our fault, Erik's and mine. Did we do something wrong that made you have such guilt feelings? Was it something in the way we brought you up? We were on your side, we would always be on your side, didn't you understand that? How could you believe that anyone would judge you because you had finally found love in your life? I get so angry at you for being so stupid that you only wanted to run away from everything. I just don't understand how you could do that to Axel. And why didn't you tell us how bad you felt, why didn't you let us help you?

'Forgive me. But there are so many questions.

'You can't stop fighting, Eva, promise me that, if nothing else then for Axel's sake. They told us that the chances are fifty-fifty for the examination tomorrow, and we mustn't give up hope yet. I'm sure that the doctor is right, the one who said that he thought you could hear us. Erik hasn't asked many doctors; apparently there's a doctor at Karolinska who's a specialist in this type of injury, I think his name is Sahlstedt or Sahlgren. We've tried to get hold of him but he seems to be on holiday this week and next. They said we should call him when he comes back.

'Dear Eva, you have to keep fighting, you have so much to live for. If you knew how grateful I am that he was with you, that he managed to rescue you. I don't think I've ever seen a man love anyone so devotedly. In the midst of all this I'm so thankful that you have him, that however things go tomorrow, the two of you managed to have the time together that you did.

'It feels a bit easier for us to know that you had a chance to experience it even though you did what you did. And that he is here with you. All the time.'

'Is there anything else you need tonight?'

It was the night nurse standing in the doorway. One hand held a tray of pill cups and the other had a firm grip on the door handle. She looked stressed.

'No thanks, we'll be fine now. Isn't that right, Eva?'

The last dregs of gruel ran through the probe into her stomach, and he stroked her brow lightly.

'Good night, then. And if I don't see you before the end of my shift, good luck in the morning.'

'Thanks.'

She smiled and closed the door behind her. He liked the staff better here at Huddinge Hospital. They knew how to appreciate his efforts and openly showed their admiration at his devotion.

Forty-three days.

And tomorrow the final examination would begin. Tiny electrodes would be inserted and would measure one last time whether the activity in her brain had increased.

In a few days they would know.

He took her hand to drive away the worry that was trying to get to him.

'Everything will be fine, darling. We're fine where we are.'

Then he pulled back the covers and raised up the

light-blue County Council Hospital gown, took the skin lotion out of the bedside table, drew a white stripe along her left leg. With even strokes he massaged the calf, continuing across the knee and further towards the groin.

'Your mother is really a fantastic woman. I'm so glad she and I are getting along so well.'

He carefully lifted her leg, put one hand behind her knee and bent it cautiously several times.

'Good, Eva.'

He went round the bed and drew another stripe on the other leg.

'Did you hear that we were talking about letting Axel come along sometime too? But she's probably right, we ought to wait for the results of the EEG first, so we know what to tell him. It might be best if I met him somewhere else before we see each other here. Maybe I should take him to Gröna Lund amusement park, would he like that? Or maybe Skansen would be better?'

He straightened out her leg, arranged it on the bottom sheet and drew his index finger across her cheek. Reached for the brush and ran it a few times through her hair.

'So, my love, now you look fine. Is there anything else you want me to do before we go to sleep?'

He took off his T-shirt and trousers, folded them and placed them on the visitor's chair. Then he reached out to turn off the bed lamp but hesitated. Stopped and looked at her, letting his gaze follow the contours of her body under her gown.

'My God, how beautiful you are.'

The calm he longed for came over him. Yet another

whole night's sleep without the compulsion being able to get to him.

So grateful.

Carefully he lay down on his side next to her, pulled the covers over them and cupped his hand over one breast.

'Good night, my darling.'

Gently he pressed his crotch against her left thigh and felt the growing arousal, remembering her hands that once so matter-of-factly had sought out his secrets.

He wanted only one thing.

Only one.

That she would hold him and tell him that he never had to be afraid any more.

Never be alone again.

'Don't be afraid, my love, I'm here with you, always.'

He would never leave her.

Never ever.

'I love you.'

SHADOW

KARIN ALVTEGEN

'It will keep you reading under the duvet during the small hours' *Daily Mail*

Gerda Persson has lain dead for three days. Her life seems to have been quite ordinary – until the freezer in her home is opened. It is full of books, neatly stacked and wrapped in clingfilm, a thick layer of ice covering them – all by the same prize-winning author, all with handwritten dedications to Gerda.

What story do these books have to tell? And what is their connection to a young boy found abandoned in an amusement park? *Shadow* is an utterly compelling novel of dark family secrets, murder and betrayal, which will keep you gripped until its final, thrilling revelations.

£7.99

ISBN 978 1 84767 171 4

ISBN 978 1 84767 478 4

www.canongate.tv

MISSING

KARIN ALVTEGEN

'Alvtegen powerfully evokes Sibylia's sense of
persecution and conveys what it means to live
as an outsider, without ever compromising
this compulsive thriller' *Metro*

When a serial killer strikes, a homeless woman
finds herself in the wrong place at the wrong time,
framed for horrifying murders that she didn't
commit. On the run and living by her wits, can she
avoid capture long enough to prove her innocence?

Missing is a gripping race against the clock, and a
thrilling story of secrets, deceptions and obsessions.

£7.99

ISBN 978 0 85786 022 4

ISBN 978 1 84767 688 7

www.canongate.tv